PROGRAMMED FOR

PLEASURE

BY C'ANN INMAN

© INMAN BOOKS LLC 2025

2ND (REVISED) EDITION

INMAN BOOKS

INFINITE POSSIBILITIES

A woman's pleasure is a sacred affair.

Her body a temple.

Her moans a melody.

Desire dances under her skin.

Hot and alive to the touch.

Prologue

Both men could clearly hear the woman's moans through the intercom. Her breathing was harsh and uneven. Her voice trembled. And she was repeatedly telling someone to fuck her. Loudly.

The sounds coming out of the speaker were at odds with the room the two men resided. They were surrounded by equipment that cost thousands of dollars. It was tidy but cramped. Many machines cluttered the small space. A digital readout scanned the woman's vitals and reported back every ten seconds. A recorder caught every moan, every breath, and every word.

Colin chuckled and shook his head. "Why don't you put the visual on?" He reached down for the switch when Ethan smacked his hand.

"Reprobate." Ethan shook his head. "I want this test to be strictly audio."

"Pity." Colin tapped the speaker in front of them on the desk. "I would personally like to see our test subject enjoy herself."

"Jesus, Colin! This is science, you freak." Ethan rolled his eyes at his best friend and boss. "Just because you're a damn voyeur doesn't mean you negate the science of this."

"Right." Colin drew the word out and arched his eyebrow. "You've got to be fucking kidding. You don't like seeing a woman orgasm? Jesus. Who's the freak now?"

Ethan was spared the indignity of answering. A minute later, the test subject, clearly disheveled but smiling, walked out of the room she had been in.

Her bleach blonde hair was mussed, and there was a healthy blush all over her skin. The black miniskirt was hiked up on her legs, and her white blouse was unbuttoned down to her stomach. Her black heels dangled over her fingers.

She walked on shaking legs over to Ethan and fairly purred, "You ever need another test subject, sugar, give me a call." She winked and staggered toward the lab door.

"Thanks, Candi!" Ethan turned to make notations on his clipboard when Colin's laughter stopped him.

"Candi? You're shitting me, right?"

Ethan frowned, his blue eyes flashing. "No. Candi with an 'i'. Says so right here." He tapped the clipboard again.

"Ethan." Colin reached over and took the clipboard out of his friend's hand. "This Candi woman." His brown eyes were kind. "Where exactly did you find her?"

"Somewhere downtown." Ethan gestured vaguely. "I forget exactly. I was trying to find a test subject. And then she approached me." His light blue eyes lit. "That's right. She asked if I was looking for someone. I told her I was. And then I explained what I wanted. She was more than happy to accompany me."

"And you paid her..." Colin's sentence trailed off.

"Three hundred." Ethan raked his hand through his short red hair. "Listen. You said it was okay."

"I know, friend of mine." Colin clapped his friend on the shoulder. "But I don't know how the study will look when people find out we hired hookers to test it."

"Hookers?" Ethan slapped his hand on the white desk. His eyes shot to the door that Candi exited from. Realization slammed through him. "Fuck me. Candi's a hooker."

"Yes, bro. And odds are that she would have fucked you if you hadn't shown her to the lab room."

3

"Son of a bitch." Ethan's voice was small and defeated. "I don't know why she couldn't have just said something."

"I know it's been a while." Colin shook his head. "But, Ethan, you seriously have to get out more. What did you tell her?"

"I told her that I needed a woman to experiment with. And that I had a room." He paused and groaned. "Back at the lab." Ethan's voice trailed off. "Fuck."

Colin held up his hands. "No harm. Isn't this thing about ready to be unleashed on the masses anyway?"

"Sure." Ethan's blue eyes grew dim.

Colin patiently waited while Ethan's brilliant mind processed the facts. He was constantly amazed that his friend could stuff so many facts into his head. It was the day-to-day stuff that kicked Ethan's ass. Such as accidentally picking up a hooker.

Ever since high school, the two boys had been inseparable. As opposite as could be, they complemented each other. Colin was the ladies' man. Charismatic. Handsome. Worldly. Ambitious.

Ethan was brilliant but introverted. And people weren't a necessity in his world. Unless they were test subjects.

And now fifteen years later, they were going to introduce a device that would make their competitors green with envy and generally piss them off. Colin grinned. Those poor bastards didn't have Ethan.

"I think we can get away with it. File for a temporary license. I still don't know how we're going to pull this off with the test subject outside the lab."

"Trust me, Ethan." Colin's grin was wide and knowing. "I have it all under control."

Chapter 1

Meg held a vibrator in each hand. The left hand was wrapped around a purple member with realistic veins up and down the sides. It was roughly eight inches long and of average width. Her right hand gripped a pink dildo that was easily nine inches and a little larger around. She glanced at her left hand. Then her right. With a shrug, she put the purple dildo back and walked to the counter with the pink.

"Cash or charge?" The young man behind the counter scooped up the toy and popped some batteries into it. At the sound of the loud humming, he smiled satisfactorily and popped the batteries back out. "Need these?"

"No thanks." Meg grinned. "I have my own."

"Wise woman." He rang up the total and took Meg's credit card. He swiped it and waited for the receipt to print.

Meg took the pen he offered and signed her name.

She watched the young man put her toy into a bag and then hand it to her.

"Enjoy."

"Always." Meg's smile was wide as she waved on the way out. The wind blew her ebony hair into her face, and she tucked it back with a grimace.

It was spring, but there was still a bite to the air that had her teeth clenching. She opted for a yellow jacket today over jeans and a blue Henley. She was going to pull her shoulder-length sable hair into a ponytail, but she thought her ears would freeze. Her blue eyes watered slightly as she unlocked her small, blue car and ducked inside.

Meg shivered slightly as she cranked up the air and waited. The warm air blew up on the window and defrosted it. She reached over and opened her bag again. The pink dildo lay there, and she picked up the box to look at the manufacturer and price again. She brought out her notebook and noted both.

Erica would be pleased. She wanted Meg to try and test a product at least once a week. Possibly twice, if time allowed. Then she would compile the data and issue her findings. *Erica's Erotica Findings* was one of the hottest sites on the web. And all of Meg's hard work was published on a weekly basis.

Both Erica and Meg decided the content of the site. Erica ran it, but Meg managed the business side. And that was in addition to her regular job as a tutor to local high school students. Money wasn't an issue for her. Her parents had seen to it that she was taken care of before they were lost so carelessly when she was nineteen. Meg didn't have to work. But she needed something to do with all that free time.

She pulled out of the adult toy store parking lot and back onto the highway. Erica asked her to make the forty-five minute trip instead of going to the local adult toy store. Too many people could see her and put two and two together. And in their small town, too many people liked to put their nose in everyone else's business.

Meg snorted as she thought of all the times she drove by the local adult shop and noted few cars there. But come late Friday evening and through the weekend, she could just make out the full parking lot through the fence.

She cranked up the heater and the radio as she drove toward home. Erica was receiving a lot of emails about expanding the site to include more product testing and ratings. Meg remembered the conversation well.

"C'mon, Meg. Just a couple more a week."

"Hire another person." Meg's tone was hard. "Listen, Erica. You know I adore you. I'd do anything for you.

And it's not like this is a hardship, but," she looked hard at her friend, "this ol' body can only take so much stimulation. And if I play with the toys too often, I actually lose some of the pleasure."

"Really?"

Meg rolled her eyes. "Honey." She patted Erica's hand. "Yes. How about you either jump in and decide to help, or you hire more people?"

Erica's brown eyes were puzzled. "You lose pleasure?"

"Overstimulation," Meg explained.

"Oh." Erica frowned as she thought of the ramifications. "Maybe I'll look into hiring someone part-time." She walked off mumbling about classified ads.

Meg laughed in remembrance. Erica didn't care much for sex. In fact, that's why she was so adamant about starting the site. She wanted to give women such as herself the tools to find good, healthy ways to give themselves pleasure. The last long-term relationship Erica was in ended almost a year ago. And she hadn't taken up with anyone since.

But the website was amazing. Women from all over the world were interested in the latest adult toys. They wanted knowledge. And Erica's site filled the void. She rated the toys with moans. One moan was a warning that it wasn't worth the money. But four moans was an indicator that the woman would have a pleasurable experience.

Meg glanced over in her passenger seat at the pink vibrator again. She pulled it out of the box and ran her hands over the contour of it. She licked her lips as she thought of it inside her, purring away. Her hips arched up in the seat, and she told herself to get a grip. The last thing she needed was to get in an accident or run off the side of the road while fantasizing about playing with herself.

It had been four days. Meg wasn't lying when she told Erica about overstimulation. She always waited between three and four days to try out the next product. And by the time she was ready for a trial run, her body needed that feeling. The absolute release.

Meg touched the vibrator again and ran her pointer finger over the tip of it. *What would it feel like? Will my body clench tightly around it while I come over and over again? Or would it be a one-hit wonder?* She shifted in her seat and told herself to wait. Another fifteen minutes, and she would be home. Then she could slide the vibrator between her legs and ease the ache.

Erica envied her. Meg could see it in her eyes every time she brought in another report. Her friend's sex drive was nothing compared to Meg's. All through college, the two women roomed together. Erica had a boyfriend, but

Meg was the one who had the orgasms. She remembered playing with herself in the shower one day when Erica walked in to use the bathroom. Her moans must have been louder than she thought.

Erica waited until Meg stepped out, and then she asked her roommate. Meg patiently explained what she was doing and told Erica where to stand and what to do. Fifteen minutes later, Erica came out with an awed expression on her face. Her whole body was flushed, and she blinked at Meg.

"I didn't know."

From then on, the girls had open discussions about sex and desire. Meg took psychology classes. Erica worked for a general degree, not really sure what she wanted to pursue. After Meg lost her parents, they became even closer. Their senior year was filled with ideas about how they could work together. And finally Erica approached Meg with the idea of the website. It would play to both their strengths. And financially, it would bring in a nice income.

Meg financed it initially, but Erica had long since paid off the debt. And they continued to work together to help other women feel what they should when having sex. The all-elusive orgasm.

Meg took her exit and drove the next five minutes with her hands wrapped tightly around the vibrator. Her nipples peaked against her shirt, and she told herself she could wait. She didn't want to cheapen the first experience with a quickie on the side of the road. She took her hand off the vibrator and slid it under her shirt and over her right breast.

Longing spread through her body, and she stroked and plucked the hardened nipple. Her legs spread of their own volition, and Meg was thankful she could see her driveway up ahead.

The two-story townhouse rose gracefully into the sky. Wraparound porches on both stories had lawn furniture, still covered and protected from the elements. The wooden shutters on the house were closed and gave the house a look of privacy. Four windows faced out on the second story. And a huge oak door with windows on both sides was on the first.

Meg parked her car in the garage and circled back around the front. She absentmindedly noticed that the plants were still covered. She'd have to watch the weather to see if it would be okay to uncover them soon. The large red maple in the front yard swayed gently with the wind. It was a gift from her father to her mother when they found out they were pregnant with her. Meg ran her hands along the side of it on the way to her front porch.

She quickly unlocked the front door and shut it behind her. The heater was on, and she hurriedly shed her jacket. It fell haphazardly on the floor. Meg looked to the left at the staircase and then to the right. She could either run up to her bedroom or simply play in the study. The ache grew stronger, and Meg veered off to the right.

A large red and gold throw rug with gold tassels lay in front of the fireplace. Meg walked over to the desk and slid out the drawer which held all her batteries. She fitted them inside and turned the toy back on. The buzz filled the room, and she smiled.

Her pussy was already wet and willing. Meg undid her jeans and slid them down her legs. She kicked off her shoes and then her jeans after them.

The buzz of the vibrator in her hand had her closing her eyes and praying for some semblance of self-control. She was supposed to be a woman who was trying this for the first time. Meg breathed in and out slowly, steadying herself. Her right hand brought the vibrator against her panties, and her breath hissed out. After she turned the vibrator down a notch, she sank to the rug.

With her back flat against the floor, she slid her panties down to her ankles. The pink silk pooled there, and that turned Meg on even more. She bent her knees, spreading her legs farther. Her right hand moved back to her pussy and gently put the tip of the pink vibrator against herself.

Meg lowered her legs further to the side as she slowly stroked the tip against her hard clit. She moved the vibrator down farther to her pussy opening, probing the slick slit. She eased it in an inch or two before bringing it out again and up to her throbbing clit.

Bracing her left hand against the rug, Meg moved her hips up to grind against the vibrator. She pretended to fuck the man of her dreams.

Meg closed her eyes and pictured him. Blond hair. Blue eyes. Massive cock. And willing mouth. Her body trembled as the sensations against her clit became more intense. Many times she fantasized about this man when she masturbated. But this time she didn't want his hard cock in her. She wanted his tongue fucking her pussy. Sucking her clit.

She moaned and turned the vibrator back up. Meg ran it over her clit again, imagining the man's mouth buried against her, pleasuring her pussy.

Then she slid the vibrator down and eased it inside herself. Her muscles clenched around it, and she closed her legs, fucking her imaginary man. Meg's hips arched over and over again until she could feel the tingle start between her legs. Her body tightened, and her nipples hardened as she continued to fuck the vibrator.

"Oh. Yes." Meg moved it faster and faster between her legs. Her breathing was ragged, and she fought to keep control. "Fuck me. Just keep fucking me." Her body shook as the first orgasm hit her. And still she continued to pump the vibrator between her legs, making sure it rubbed against her clit on every stroke. The second orgasm hit her harder, and she screamed as the pleasure rippled through her. Her legs tensed and clenched while she shuddered in orgasmic bliss.

Meg came down slowly and tried to control her breathing. Slowly in. Slowly out. She looked at the shiny, pink vibrator beside her on the rug and licked her dry lips. *Three and a half moans. Easy.* She rarely gave out fours. But this little jewel did the job nicely.

"Shit." Meg sat up slowly and blinked. Her blue eyes were hazy with satisfaction. There was a nice little wet spot on the floor, and she chuckled. Her body still throbbed dully. Another couple of minutes, and she might be fully functional. Maybe.

She kicked off her panties and scooped them up to put on top of her jeans. The Henley was thrown down next.

And then her bra. Nude was best anyway. As long as it was warm.

Meg took her clothes into the laundry room. She snatched a bright purple robe off the hook and wound it around herself. Then she slid on her orange slippers and shuffled back into the study.

The pink vibrator lay on the floor, and Meg picked it up gently and took it to the bathroom. She washed it, dried it, and put it back in the box. Then it went up with the rest of the toys.

Living by herself was something she was eternally grateful for. Other people were nice, but she didn't want to have to explain herself or her actions to anyone. Being an only child fed into that independence and need for solitude. And how in the hell would she explain the closet in her study with stacks upon stacks of adult toys?

Meg slid the vibrator onto the third shelf and shut the door. She leaned against it for a second before letting her eyes scan the room. No student today for her to tutor, but she was scheduled for one tomorrow.

The room was fine except for the faint aroma of her arousal. Meg ran her hands over her large, cherry wood desk. It used to be her dad's. He kept it at his office for years. And now she did her business around it. She slid into the large brown leather seat and opened her notebook up.

"The vibrator deserves a solid three and a half moans from the tester. The size was adequate without being overwhelming, and the pleasure to be had with this toy is second to none."

Meg finished her notations and then emailed Erica. When she was through, she walked over to the fireplace and started a small fire. It crackled softly at first and then blazed when she slid two logs on top of the flames. She held out her hands and felt the warmth through her body. The scent comforting.

The room was almost mannish in its color and hues. It was a bold statement of strength and power. Reds and golds vied for attention in every accessory. The furniture was solid cherry wood and shone softly in the flickering of the fire's flames. Two bookshelves from floor to ceiling flanked the fireplace and its marble mantle. A large portrait on the wall to her right was sumptuous and inviting.

A naked woman lay resplendent on a crimson chaise chair with her back to her audience. She turned her upper body so the hint of her right breast could be seen. Long, copper tresses flowed down her back and brushed against the soft swell of her bottom. A knowing smile danced on her lips as she looked out into the room.

"Show off," Meg muttered with a smile. It was her favorite piece. She had named the woman Madeline. It somehow fit. Her parents didn't understand her fascination with it, and neither did she. But she loved it. To be so beautiful. So comfortable in her own skin. The woman in the portrait was confident. And that, in itself, was sexy to her.

Her own hair was jet black and fine. Nothing curled. And it certainly didn't gleam the way the woman's appeared to in the picture. Her curves were a little fuller. And her eyes didn't hold the same knowledge as the woman's.

Yes, Meg could give herself one hell of an orgasm. But not many men could say they had done the same. She sighed. Two men, to be exact. And she really thought one just rather lucked into it. His hand had brushed against her clit while they were having sex, and she finally brought his hand back down and had him stroke her while his cock moved in and out.

Meg shivered in the room as arousal swept through her again. She clenched her teeth against it and told herself it wasn't going to happen again so soon. The last thing she needed was to barely be able to walk when her student arrived tomorrow.

Being an "all or nothing" personality type had its share of ups and downs. When Erica first approached her with the idea about the adult toys, Meg had literally thrown herself into it. The first toy she had brought home, she played with herself three times that night. Her climaxes had lessened in intensity, and she felt hung over the next day. Moderation wasn't easy, but she had to have some.

Her hand slipped between the folds of her robe and to her bare pussy. She slid a finger down between her lips and felt the moisture again. Meg bit her lip. One of two choices. More masturbation or a cold shower. She looked outside and shivered. Screw the cold shower. As long as she didn't use the electric toys all the time, her clit wouldn't become desensitized.

Meg undid the sash of her robe, and let it fall open to reveal her bare body underneath. She licked two fingers of her left hand and let them trail slowly down her body. Her right hand came across and pulled at her sensitive nipples. Time to bring back her fantasy man.

What would he taste like? What would he feel like? Meg threw her head back as her left hand parted her legs and found the sensitive nub between them. She stroked it softly while she imagined her lips trailing across her man and down his body. His hands would fist in her hair as she moved down to take his hard cock into her mouth.

She licked her lips at the thought. Meg could almost feel his muscled ass in her hands as she worked her mouth up and down his shaft, sucking his length into her willing mouth. Then he would lay her down and ease that hard cock into her eager body. Meg shuddered as her body tightened. She bucked her hips against her hand at the thought of him ramming into her over and over again. His mouth on her nipples, sucking them while he slid in and out of her.

Meg cried out as her knees buckled, and she barely caught herself on the desk before she fell. Her body trembled as aftershocks ripped through her body.

"Wow." She sighed as the last of her pleasure tapered off. Her hands shook a little as she brought the robe back together again. *And if that didn't do it, then too damn bad. No more playing today.* She couldn't take it.

* * * *

Ethan carefully picked up the box and set it on the desk in front of him. It looked like a black cigar box. Plain. Simple. It was anything but. He tapped the lid and smiled as the cover eased up and let him touch the pieces inside. Microchips and mazes of wires crisscrossed from wall to wall in the box. Ethan looked around until he found the one he was looking for, and then he carefully spliced it and added the final touch. He was almost ready.

"I've got her!" Colin slammed through the door with his fist pumping.

Ethan swiveled around to glare at his best friend. "I'm going to alter your coffeemaker if you do that stupid shit again. I'm performing a delicate operation." He motioned with his head back toward the box.

"Sorry, man." Colin sank into a spare chair and watched Ethan work his magic.

Ethan's light blue eyes traced wire after wire until he found what he wanted. His impossibly large hands moved carefully while he worked on his masterpiece. When the lid shut again, at last, Colin arched an eyebrow.

"It's okay for me to breathe now?"

Ethan rolled his eyes. "Listen, smart-ass, that was it. We're ready to roll. I hope you kept your part of the deal."

"As I was saying, before you rudely told me to shut the fuck up." Colin paused to wink at his friend. "I found her."

"Her?" Ethan repeated.

"Her. Shit, Ethan. Keep up. The test subject." Colin stood quickly and paced. His energy fairly bounced off the walls. "I got to thinking. How in the hell are we going to find someone who will do this study justice? And I'm not renting any more hookers."

Ethan casually flipped his friend off and waited for the rest of the story.

"So, I pulled a few strings. Made a few calls. And what did I find?"

"A sex addict in the yellow pages?"

Colin's eyebrows shot up. "Go get laid, man. I mean it. You're cranky." He paused for effect. "I found a woman who frequents adult toy stores. She needs to have a fucking tab there. You wouldn't believe some of the shit she's bought." He rubbed his hands together. "So then I started thinking…"

"And you came by this information how?"

"All in good time." Colin's story wouldn't be denied. "We're going to set up a contest. A rigged contest, but nonetheless. And this chick will win." He raked his hands through his hair and laughed. "She'll think she's won the lottery. And then we'll have her sign a bunch of consent papers. We'll slip in a few extras, and she'll be ours."

"The chick?"

"Chick. Test subject." Colin waved his hand around. "What the fuck ever. The nympho."

"And you came by this information how?" Ethan repeated. "Are we going to get sued?"

"No way." Colin shook his head emphatically. "The clerk at the store is a friend's brother's cousin. He sees her in there all the time. It's absolutely perfect."

"Perfect." Ethan savored the word as his hand rested on the black box. A test subject who would appreciate all his hard work.

Chapter 2

Erica slapped her hand on the desk. "I cannot believe you're being so selfish."

Meg calmly sat back in her chair and looked at her friend. "Same goes."

"Dammit, Meg," Erica railed. "I can't find another test subject in this kind of time. It's not like I can take out a classified ad. I already tried that." She pushed her auburn hair back behind her ear. "Got a bunch of fucking lunatics wanting to show me what they were actually doing with the merchandise." Her blue eyes sought out her friend's. "I couldn't eat for two days."

"The guilt's not working."

"Give me a month to find some new people." Erica's eyes pleaded with hers. "A month, Meg. I don't understand why you need a sabbatical anyway."

Meg stood up abruptly and walked over to the window. She looked out and saw people scurrying up and down the sidewalks, huddled against the chill. Adults. Children. Couples.

"I'm becoming too attached to the idea of my fantasy man."

"Oh." The word was short and confused.

Meg turned back around and smiled. "I know you don't understand that, Erica. But you have to respect it. I like orgasms. Shit, I love them. But I'd like to have someone else's hands on me besides my own. A man's mouth. A man's body. Not just my imaginary fuck."

"Oh."

She laughed at the puzzlement still on her friend's face. "I just need a little break to find someone to fill this need. Then I'll go back to being your guinea pig, okay?"

"Is it really different?"

Meg sat down and put her hands across the desk to clasp her friend's. "Honey, someday you'll find the man who can make your body sing. And then the buzz of your toy will somehow become less than enchanting.

"You'll give me a month?"

"One month. And then I'll need a month for myself.

"Done." Erica tapped her cheek thoughtfully. "A man who can make my body sing, huh?"

"At the top of its lungs."

* * * *

Meg drove to the toy store while a smile played on her lips. This would be the last trip for a while. Then she'd hit the club scene and see if she could find someone who would fulfill her needs in the corporeal sense. She had tried once to hook up with a professor from the college but found he wasn't to her liking. Being in the missionary position all the time was boring. And when she suggested something a little more risqué, he balked. And that's when she was done. She parked and walked inside the store, humming.

The sign hit her first. It was a huge, red, throbbing heart. "Your Pleasure" was stenciled in white across it in large letters. Then a large red arrow tapered down from the heart to a clear box overflowing with papers.

She turned to look at the kid behind the counter. "What the hell is this?"

He hurried toward her. "We have a supplier running a contest. The ultimate sex toy. For women only." He picked up an entry form and pen to hand to her. "You can enter today. The drawing is Friday."

Meg handed the pen and paper back. "That's okay. Really."

The boy's face dropped. "Hey! Are you kidding? The ultimate sex toy? You'd pass up a chance for that?" He held the supplies out to her again. His eyes were pleading.

Meg took them with a sigh. "I never win these things." She filled out her information and dropped it into the box. Her hand tapped the box. "Looks like a lot of women are in search of this toy."

The boy grinned and winked. "But I think today is your lucky day."

* * * *

Meg took her purchase back out to her car. She had purchased a small, clitoral stimulator and some flavored lube. The flavored lube was wishful thinking. How she wished she had someone to taste or someone to taste her. Her hands crept over to her bag, and she pulled out the clitoral stimulator.

It was small and pink with tiny nubs across the surface. It actually came with straps in case she wanted to wear it under her clothes. The thought tickled her. *An orgasm to go.* She actually purchased batteries this time. Meg switched on the stimulator and ran her fingers across it while she pulled out of the parking lot. Maybe she'd pop in an adult movie when she got home and try her newest addition out.

The stimulators worked best for her if she rocked her body back and forth against them while mimicking sex. Her thumb traced the nubs, and her skin broke out in goose bumps.

"Dammit," she muttered, turning the toy off and hurriedly tucking it back in the bag. It would be nice to not be aroused by plastic for a while.

* * * *

The phone call came exactly three days later. Meg held up her hand and apologized to the student in front of her. "I'll be right back." She hurried to the kitchen and picked up the phone.

"Meg White?"

"Yes." Meg frowned a little. She only used that name for certain occasions. Rarely did she use her full given name.

"You filled out an entry form for the ultimate adult toy?"

"Yes."

"Congratulations!"

Meg's jaw dropped. "Pardon me?"

"You've won!" The voice on the other end of the phone was exuberant and jovial. "All we need you to do is to come to our offices and pick up the prize. We'll be open all day."

"That's nice." Meg tried to catch her breath. She shot a glance back toward her study. "I'm busy today. Will you be there tomorrow?"

"Yes." The tone lost some of its exuberance. "You don't want to pick it up today?"

"I have appointments. Give me the information, and I'll be down tomorrow." A thought occurred to her. "There isn't going to be any publicity or anything, is there?"

"I promise that absolutely no publicity will surround you picking up the device."

"Okay." Meg shook her head. "Imagine that," she murmured.

"Excuse me?"

"Nothing." Meg quickly wrote down the information and thanked the man. She hung up the phone with a perplexed look on her face. She just apparently won the ultimate sex toy. *How ironic was that?*

* * * *

Colin hung up the phone with a frown. Ethan waited expectantly for him to speak. After a minute he tapped the desk.

"Well? When is she coming down?"

"Tomorrow." Colin shook his head. "I don't understand it. I thought she would jump at the chance."

"I'm not going to be here tomorrow. I told you that." Ethan's blue eyes darkened to a stormy sea. "And that means you have to deal with this whole thing yourself. And do you even know how to show her to use it?"

"Ethan, chill out. I've got it covered. You go and listen to your little conference. Everything will be fine here." Colin brought out a sheaf of papers. "I'll just inundate the woman with papers. Have her sign them and show her the door. She asked about publicity."

"Smart," Ethan commented. "I heard your response. Even smarter."

"Of course." Colin's brown eyes were cool. "No publicity until she turns the toy back in."

* * * *

Meg dressed carefully the next morning. She wore tan, casual slacks and a nondescript crème shirt. She took a wig out of her closet and slipped it over her hair. The short, dark curls framed her face and completely changed her look. Then she slipped the sunglasses on. The man on the phone said there would be no publicity, but she learned long ago not to trust people who had something to gain.

She painted her face with dark colors, and changed her skin color to two shades darker. Meg was almost unrecognizable. It was a trick she saw her mother use many times to escape the house for a while. It was always nice to step outside of her boundaries. Outside of her expectations.

She grabbed a plain brown purse and slung it over her shoulder. *Ready to go.* Meg grabbed her keys and readied herself for the day ahead. She had warred back and forth with herself about telling Erica and then decided not to. Not very long ago, she'd pitched a fit in Erica's office to not be near plastic. And now she was going to pick some up.

The drive took fifteen minutes, and Meg checked her make-up one last time before she stepped out of her car and into the massive, brick building. She changed her walk to a slower, more sedate pace. And then she stepped inside the building.

A man immediately spotted her and hurried over. Meg watched him behind her dark glasses.

He was a businessman. That was obvious. From the expensive haircut and cut of his clothes, to the knowing smile that leapt to his face. He knew what his looks could do. And they were stunning. Easily six three and powerfully built. Dark, chocolate eyes looked down at her with a smile. Perfect white teeth blinded her.

"Miss White?" he asked.

"Yes." She injected a slight accent into her voice and inclined her head.

"Come this way." He held out his arm, and she looped hers through his. The heat of his body moved through her thin jacket and shirt. And he smelled clean and woodsy.

Meg followed him to the elevators and up five floors. When the doors opened, he allowed her to step out first. She looked behind her and found he studied her.

"Colin Price." He held out his hand, and she took it. His fingers closed over hers with a slight squeeze.

"Pleasure."

"Are your eyes bothering you?"

"No." The word was short and asked for no comment.

"Ms. White, I assured you there would be no publicity. But I can respect your desire for privacy."

"Thank you." Meg followed him into another room with a small table and two chairs. On the table was a small black box and a pair of earrings.

Colin brought out a stack of papers and set them in front of Meg. "I need you to sign these. Standard consent forms. The like." He watched as she thumbed through most of them, reading a line or two. He began to sweat as she moved farther and farther down into them. She stopped abruptly and let them fall back together.

"A pen?"

Meg signed her name several times and initialed in at least twenty different places. When she finished, Colin divided the papers and gave her half.

"These are yours," he explained.

She took them and tapped the table. "I'm assuming that the ultimate sex toy is tucked into that box?" And then she picked up the earrings. "Are these a consolation prize?"

"Hardly." She watched a slow smile spread across his face. "These are part of the toy."

"Please explain."

Colin picked up the black box. "This is the ultimate sex toy. But you need these," he touched the earrings, "to access it. You noted on the entry form that your ears are pierced?"

"Yes." Meg touched her lobes. "But I don't wear earrings often."

"No matter." Colin touched the box lightly. "This technology is cutting edge. I need you to take these both home and use them immediately. We have a 1-800 number you can call and leave a message on. You don't need to talk to anyone directly. But we'd like your feedback."

She frowned lightly. "And that's it?"

"The instructions are inside this envelope." He handed her a plain brown manila envelope. "Read them. Follow them. I look forward to your opinion, Ms. White."

"Thank you." Meg tucked everything into the bag Colin provided. She stood to walk out the door when his voice stopped her.

"Congratulations, Ms. White. I think you'll be pleased you entered our contest that day."

She nodded and hurried back out to her car. Meg started it and drove back to her house quickly. Curiosity was making her edgy. *What could possibly be the ultimate sex toy? What would it feel like? Look like?*

Meg pulled into her driveway and unlocked her front door. The wig flew off, followed by her jacket and shoes. Her ebony hair fell softly to her shoulders, and she shook it out.

Walking quickly, she took the precious container upstairs and into her bedroom. The soft blues of the room soothed her immediately. A sky-blue comforter and pillows decorated her queen-size bed. Blue chiffon curtains brushed up against large windows that opened to let a soft breeze in. Her oak vanity was littered with the make-up she had used to disguise herself. And her wardrobe was still half open. A large oak bookshelf was to the right of her bed, and she wondered vaguely if she had room to keep the box there. But in the end, she settled it in beside her on the nightstand with her lamp.

Meg took a shower and then walked back into her bedroom. She slipped the small, silver studs into her hand and then opened the instructions. She read though them halfway and then turned the black box on.

A man appeared.

Meg shrieked and shot off the bed, scrambling to find something to cover herself with. She snatched a small, blue robe out of her closet and thrust her hands through the sleeves, belting it tightly.

And still, the man stood there. She walked slowly toward him and tried to touch his sleeve, but her hand passed right through him.

"Son of a bitch," she whispered. Meg picked one of her slippers off and threw it at the figure. It flew right through him. He never blinked. She pressed her hand to her chest and was relieved to find her heart hadn't somehow burst from her chest. *A projection. Had to be.*

Meg walked closer to him and studied him from every angle. He was tall. She was five eight, and he had quite a few inches on her. His eyes were brown. Nondescript. As was his hair. He could have had the same haircut as millions of men. He wore jeans and a white T-shirt with the sleeves rolled. That tickled her for some reason. James Dean came to mind. His features were rather bland. Nothing that seemed to jump out at her and demand attention.

She circled him slowly, surprised she could see his features from every angle. And still he stood there lifeless.

Meg came back round to the bed and picked up the instructions again. Served her right for not reading them all the way through the first time. *Shit.* She almost had a coronary. When she finished reading all the way down, she slid the two stud earrings into her ears and waited.

"Hello."

Meg jumped. The man's deep voice echoed through her room, and she blinked rapidly. She moved closer and peered into his face. His features somehow seemed to come alive.

"Hello," she responded.

The man smiled easily. "What's your name?"

"Margaret. But you can call me Meg."

"Meg." He repeated the name slowly, as if sipping in every syllable. "I like it." His white teeth flashed in his face, and she felt an answering response on her own.

"What's your name?" Meg looked at him curiously.

"What do you want it to be?" The man quirked an eyebrow and shot her a devilish grin.

Her jaw dropped. "You're kidding me, right? Is there a camera somewhere around here?" She glanced around the room as if waiting for a dozen people to burst from her closet.

He moved closer, and Meg swore she could feel the heat from him. "What do you want my name to be, Meg?"

"Derek," she murmured. "I like the name Derek."

He accepted the words with a nod. "And do you like my eyes?" He touched them gently. "Or my hair?"

"I prefer blond hair and blue eyes."

Meg's jaw dropped as the man metamorphosed in front of her. The dark hair faded into light with barely a second between shades. And his eyes faded lighter and lighter until she swore she could see herself in them.

"Wow." Her heart raced. The image before her was so close to the one in her head that she had a problem breathing for a couple of seconds.

"Is this better?" His deep voice washed over her.

"It's perfect." Meg's voice was breathless. She snapped out of her reverie for a minute. "How does this work? Do we just talk back and forth? You tell me what I want to hear?" She reached down to put her hand beneath her robe when his stopped her.

"No way," she whispered. Meg looked down and saw his hand around her arm. She brought her other hand up

37

and met warm skin. "I can feel you." She pinched herself and winced. "Am I dreaming?"

"No, Meg. You can feel me. And I can feel you." His hands reached up to touch the earrings. "These help."

Her left hand came up again and touched his wrist. He was warm. Alive. Meg shook her head. "It's impossible."

Derek wound his fingers through her hair and jerked her head lightly to the side. He brought his mouth down closer. Closer. Until Meg thought she would die from waiting. And then his lips touched her neck. Softly. On her pulse point. Her fingers dug into his arm as she gasped.

"You like that." The words were certain.

Meg blinked. "Yes." She was still trying to recover from the feel of his mouth on her skin. "I did." Understanding lit in her eyes. "But you somehow knew that." She pulled back and looked him in the eye. "How do you know?"

"Your body tells me." He touched the earrings again.

"Holy shit." Meg shook her head as her blue eyes widened. "You *are* the ultimate sex toy."

She watched Derek closely. Her body was aroused by the simple touch of this projection's mouth on her neck.

And really, that's all he was. A projection. And somehow, he could read her body's responses through the earrings.

"Come here." Her voice shook slightly, and she worked to steady it.

Derek moved closer, but his arms stayed by his sides. "What do you want?"

"I want you." Meg held out her hand and felt Derek's slide into hers. She clasped it tightly and brought him around to the side of the bed. She sank slowly onto the mattress, and Derek moved down beside her, his knees on either side of her body.

Meg wound her arms around his neck, pulling him down farther to fit his body next to hers. On top of hers. And she savored every inch of him.

Her right leg moved up and hooked around his waist while Derek brought his mouth down to hers. Slowly.

And when his lips touched hers, Meg sighed. *So much better than plastic.* His right hand moved down her body and opened up her robe. He found her right breast and brought it out from under the robe. And then he lifted his head and looked at her.

Meg felt desire slam through her with a fierceness that scared her. And then he lowered his head and took her nipple into his mouth, still looking at her.

He began to suck gently and then harder as she wound her hands through his hair and arched her body into his. His left hand moved the robe aside and cupped her other breast. Derek's thumb traced lazily over the hardened nipple, and she tugged him closer.

"Please." The moan escaped her throat without her realizing she was speaking aloud.

He brought his mouth up and licked his lips. Meg shuddered in need. Her body throbbed hotly, and she wanted him inside her. *Now. Please.* And then his hand moved. And what she thought was pure desire changed. Grew. Multiplied.

Derek's hand trailed down her bare stomach to her pussy, gently parting her lips with his finger and finding her hard clit. He watched her face intently, and Meg found that even more exciting. She spread her legs farther. Wanting. Needing. And still he stroked her. His fingers slick with her body's need.

"Fuck me, Derek. Fuck me." The words were a command, and she arched up against him again. She needed him inside her. His cock. Pushing up against her. Stroking her pussy. Meg shuddered again. "Please."

And then Derek's clothes seemed to disintegrate off of him. And all there was now was skin against skin. Meg traced his collarbone with her hand and brought his mouth down to hers. Heat poured off of her. His tongue traced every curve of her mouth and plunged deep inside. And then he caught her gasp as she felt his hard cock push inside her.

Her hands clenched at his shoulders and then moved down, scraping her nails across his back.

Meg locked her legs around his waist as Derek moved deeper and deeper. He seemed to adjust to her seamlessly. Faster. Slower. She felt his hand move down between them again to run his fingers across her swelling clit. And then his fingers matched the movement of his cock, and Meg arched against him.

She cried out as wave after wave shook her. Her spine felt as if it would snap from the intensity. Meg's body shook and trembled as the pleasure lessened gradually.

"Oh shit." The words shook in her dry throat as she rolled over and looked at the naked man beside her.

Derek watched her quietly for a second, and then he spoke. "Is there anything else you want or need?"

Meg walked on trembling knees and hit the switch on the black box. Her ultimate sex toy disappeared without a trace. She turned and fell back on the bed again. The sheets tore all to hell, and there were damp places where she knew her body showed its need.

She slowly belted her robe again and walked downstairs. Her fingers trailed along the cherry banister, and she paused to tap it softly at the bottom. Meg made her way, as if in a trance, to the kitchen and poured herself a glass of water. Her hand shook slightly as she brought it to her mouth.

She had just been fucked senseless by a projection. Even now her body wanted to go another round. His mouth. His cock. Everything was perfect. Her fantasies come to life. Even his name, Derek. *Perfection. The Ultimate Sex Toy. Oh fuck.* She giggled. *They had no damn idea.*

Meg picked up the phone number off the counter and dialed it. When the electronic voice came on, she chose the right number and graded her experience on a scale of one to ten. She tried eleven, but the voice informed her that wasn't an option. That sent her off on another gale of laughter. When Meg finished pushing all the correct buttons, she hung up the phone with a smile. The salesclerk was right. It must have been her lucky day.

* * * *

Ethan blew into his office early Monday and immediately booted up his computer. The woman should have his experimental toy up and running by now. He logged on and accessed the data from the computer.

42

Numbers scrolled up continually for two minutes, and he smiled broadly. Colin wasn't kidding. Her readings were off the chart. She obviously enjoyed her encounters with the toy. He printed off the numbers and went to find Colin.

"Hey!" Ethan slid into Colin's office and threw the papers on the desk.

Colin picked up the papers and grinned. "Well, son of a bitch." He whistled low. "Our boy nailed her good, didn't he?"

Ethan rolled his eyes and snatched the papers back. "You're such a crass shit." He waved the papers around. "Not only did our test subject enjoy the toy, she absolutely had numbers that were off the charts." He shot a look to Colin. "You did good." And then curiosity got the better of him. "What did she look like?"

Colin shrugged. "Medium height. Dark brown hair. Don't know about eye color. She wore dark glasses the entire time. Slight southern accent. Fairly unremarkable."

"Except for her ability to orgasm."

Colin snatched the papers back. "Enjoyed herself, did she?" He scanned the numbers and noted they were way above norm. "You have the visual hooked in, right?"

"Go get laid," Ethan's tone was mild. He rolled up the papers and whistled happily. "We're going to get this thing off the ground yet."

"As long as the woman remains horny."

Ethan chuckled. "With these numbers, I'd say she's perpetually horny."

Colin opened his mouth, and Ethan held up his hand. "Don't even think about it." Colin's mouth snapped shut.

Ethan saluted him with the papers and left his office.

* * * *

Meg went about her business the entire weekend as if she hadn't fucked the daylights out of a projection. She covered the little black box with a scarf and told herself it was just another toy. He was just another toy. *Derek.* She squeezed her hands together and told herself to get a grip. *Now. Self-control. That's what it was all about.*

She gardened a bit on Saturday, mostly tilling up dirt and checking to see what she wanted to plant when it warmed a little. Sunday was spent browsing through her textbooks and reading.

But Monday was different. Meg woke up feeling as though if she didn't have sex right that minute, she would explode. And it was killing her. She tried everything. A cool shower. Baking cookies. Cleaning. Dusting. And nothing worked. She would find herself stock-still after

ly hopped in
the shower. She scrubbed her body and told herself she
was being silly. *Who had to get all clean and nice for
someone who couldn't smell you anyway?* Her hand
ventured down to her pussy, and she sighed. On fire. She
was on fire. The sensitive flesh throbbed beneath her
hand. She turned the shower off and towel-dried quickly.

When she took the scarf off of the box, she simply sat
and looked at it a minute. Her dream man in one
convenient container.

Meg inserted the earrings into her ears and turned the
box on. Derek appeared instantly. His clothes were the
same as last time, but he had retained his fair coloring that
she favored so much. Need poured through her.

"Meg." Derek's voice was husky in the silent room.

She spread her legs, showing him her pink pussy. She
stroked herself lightly. His eyes were immediately drawn
to the movement. Her left hand spread her lips farther
apart while she licked her right index finger and brought it

down to touch her clit. The nub swelled further against her finger.

"This is where I want your mouth."

He sank to his knees immediately and buried his mouth against her. His tongue instinctively found her clit and sucked on it while he grabbed her ass cheeks and brought her against his mouth, helping her to fuck herself against his face.

Meg grabbed his hair and spread her legs further. "Fuck me with your tongue," she demanded. "Make me come in your mouth." She rocked back and forth against him, reveling in the sensations he caused.

"Oh God." She trembled as the pleasure burst suddenly through her, and still Derek continued working his tongue against her delicate flesh. She cried out again and still he worked her pussy against his willing mouth.

Meg's body calmed after a few minutes, and she eyed Derek lazily. "You don't care what I say or do, do you?"

"No." He shook his head. "My job is to please you." His blue eyes found hers. "And did I?"

"What did the earrings tell you?"

His smile was slow and easy. "That you had two orgasms."

Meg threw back her head and laughed until tears sprang from her eyes. "Son of a bitch," she wheezed. "There's no faking now, is there?"

His light blue eyes watched her steadily.

"You're a little disconcerting." Meg reached up and grabbed his hair to tug his face closer to hers. She reached out and lightly bit his lower lip. "Do you feel desire?"

"I feel what you want me to feel."

Meg rolled over and pulled him on top of her. The solid weight of him made her smile again. So much better than the toys in her study closet. She hugged him closer and felt his cock swell against the inside of her thighs.

"And that is…" She let the question hang. And then moved her thigh so it rubbed against his hardness.

"What you want," he said, before he lowered his mouth to hers.

* * * *

Ethan collected his numbers and began to chart them. If he could show a pattern of consistent use and pleasure, they were sure to get their license and then patent. He pulled up the last sheet and cursed mildly as the numbers tapered off the bottom.

"Millions of dollars in research and a printer that can't print straight." He mumbled under his breath as he brought his data up again. And then he stilled immediately.

The needle graphic on his computer was dancing wildly across the screen. The nympho, *test subject*, Ethan silently amended, was using the toy.

His jaw dropped at a particularly sharp spike. She was giving the toy a workout. And then some. His hand wandered over to his mouse. Just a peek. One peek. He needed to know what she looked like anyway. His curiosity was sharp and relentless. And then he clicked.

A smooth ass filled the screen. And just below that, his creation's cock was pleasuring the test subject. The toy was fucking her mercilessly from behind while his right hand had disappeared between her legs.

Ethan sat back in his chair and watched the screen closely. His toy's eyes were his. That's how he designed it. To be able to see what it did. To know what it could do. And right now he watched in envy as it fucked this woman.

He flicked on the audio button and listened closely.

"I love your cock."

The words startled him so much, he almost dropped his pen. Ethan told himself to breathe. Slowly. In and out. This was research. But his cock still sprang to attention under the desk.

The toy said something, and she moaned. "Yes. Fuck me harder."

Ethan watched the toy's hands grip the woman's hips as he worked in and out faster. He tried to see the woman's face, but all he could see was sable hair. *Sable?* The thought skittered through his mind to be brought back later, as she moaned again.

"You know what I want, don't you?"

Ethan leaned in closer. "Tell me. Tell me what you want." He whispered the words as if to negate the fact he uttered them.

"I want you to keep sliding your cock in and out of my wet pussy. Make me come."

His eyes were drawn to the top of the computer screen where her vitals were being recorded. A red line climbed on the chart. Farther and farther. Ethan touched himself under the desk and told himself that he didn't need to masturbate to a test subject. But the huskiness in her voice, the words, and that damn spike were weakening him.

And then she gasped. Just a quick little inhalation before she came. And Ethan threw back his head and let himself come, too. His breathing was ragged, and he hurriedly turned off the audio and visual buttons.

"Jesus," he panted. Now he'd have to go and change his pants like some horny sixteen-year old whose date only let him go to third base. "Shit." Ethan stood and glanced down at the numbers on the chart. He could chart later. Right now he needed to get out of these clothes before Colin came in and gave him shit for doing exactly what Colin wanted to do earlier.

* * * *

Meg turned off the black box and lay back on the bed with a satisfied sigh. Her body was utterly relaxed. Pure bliss. She almost purred as she ran her hand up and down her light blue comforter. Derek did his job magnificently. And she didn't have to make small talk and chitchat after orgasm. She didn't have to stroke his ego and assure him that yes, she had come all over herself. Even though she had. She snickered softly.

Maybe she didn't need to find a real man right now. All her needs were being met by the wonderful toy she had in her little black box. Meg stood slowly and patted the box on her way downstairs. She couldn't ask for much more.

Chapter 3

Meg met Erica for lunch Wednesday and asked how her replacement was doing.

"Fine. Just fine." Erica sipped her tea and studied her friend over the menu in front of her. "She's really thrown herself into it. A kid in a candy store."

"I'm glad." Meg winked at her friend. "Are her reports satisfactory?"

"Honey," Erica drawled, "I could draw these fucking toys in my sleep. Thorough, she is."

"Are you still pissed off at me?" Meg set her menu down and looked over at Erica.

"No." Erica set her menu down, too. "Not really. And I suppose everyone needs a vacation."

The waiter came to take their orders, and Meg tapped her hand against the table.

"You have a student coming today?" Erica's brown eyes looked down at Meg's tapping hand.

"No. Not today." She took a breath. "I have a question for you."

"Shoot."

"Our website offers the ultimate in pleasure. Right?"

"Yes." Erica's brown eyes were puzzled. "That would be the intent."

"How many toys have I rated four moans?"

"Only two." Erica sipped her tea again and laughed. "The one that made you bite your own tongue. And the clitoral stimulator that hit your g-spot."

"That's right." Meg's cool blue eyes met her friends. "The Ultimate Sex Toy is a fantasy, right?"

"Are you all right?" Erica reached over and stilled Meg's hand with her own. "Something you want to talk about?"

"No." Meg shook her head briskly and smiled. "Nothing. My mind was simply wandering." She reached into her oversized brown bag and brought out her checkbook. "Do you want me to write a check to our tester through the business account?"

"Please." Erica watched Meg scribble hastily across the check and tear it off.

"Fill in her name. I'll give all the records to my accountant."

"What are you not telling me?"

Meg smiled at her friend's persistence. "Nothing, hon. Absolutely nothing."

* * * *

Meg drove home slowly. Her mind was filled with thoughts of sex, Derek, and what she was going to do about everything. She had only read through the first ten papers in her stack. Derek, dream fuck extraordinaire, was supposed to be turned in two months after she won the prize.

Two months was quite a long time to have her brains fucked out on a regular basis. She pulled into her driveway, killed the engine, and sat there tapping her fingers on the steering wheel.

She couldn't quite get a grip on what was bothering her. Everything she wanted was in a little black box on her nightstand. The simple thought of his body touching hers was enough to make her pussy wet. There were so many things she wanted to do to him and have him do to her.

Meg jumped out of her little car and hit the door at a trot. She unlocked it quickly and shut it behind her. Her jacket fell to the floor as she scurried up the stairs.

As soon as she entered the room, she stopped. Her eyes looked over at the black box. Meg walked over and sat on the edge of the bed. She picked it up slowly and put it in her lap. Her fingers stroked the top softly.

Could she have him anywhere she wanted? Or could he only function in the bedroom? Surely, she could move him around and have the same result?

Meg stripped down to the skin and carried the box into the bathroom. She started the shower and left the door open so the steam wouldn't affect whatever made the box function. When she was ready, she put the earrings in her ears and hit the switch.

Derek appeared instantly. His eyes crinkled in a smile.

"Hello, Meg."

"Hello, Derek." She moved closer and touched his chest softly. "I want you nude." Meg watched his clothes disappear with a satisfied smile. She held out her hand. "Join me in the shower."

She stepped inside and watched as he joined her. The water seemed not to affect him at all. Meg's hand reached up and touched his still-dry hair. "Amazing," she muttered.

His hand captured hers.

"What do you want?" Derek's voice was soft.

Meg turned and pressed herself up against the tiles at the back of the shower. Her nipples peaked against the cold, hard wall. She moaned and spread her legs. "I want you to eat my pussy first. On your knees, while the water hits my back. And then I want you to fuck me from behind, standing up." She looked over her shoulder at him.

He fell to his knees immediately.

Meg's breath heaved in her throat as Derek spread her legs further apart so he could obey her commands. The first touch of his mouth on her pussy lips had her fists clenching. She rubbed her body against the tiles as his tongue flicked against her pussy folds and then gently sucked on her clit. She reached down and grabbed his head with her left hand. A few minutes were all she could stand.

"Fuck me now," she rasped.

Meg felt him stand and then press his body to hers. His hand probed between her legs and found her pussy slick and ready. Derek grabbed his cock and bent her slightly, easing himself deep inside her.

She trembled against the tiles as he moved slowly in and out. His body pressed harder up against hers, and his arms moved to pin hers against the wall. And still his cock eased in and out of her.

"I like fucking you."

Meg flattened her hands against the wall as Derek began to move faster. His left hand kept her pinned as his right moved down between her legs again. His fingers unerringly found her clit and stroked it as his cock pumped in and out of her.

"Your pussy tastes so good." Derek's breath eased across her ear. His tongue flickered across her neck in the same way he stroked her clit.

Meg shook as she felt the beginnings of her orgasm. And then Derek sped up until she was crying out, telling him to fuck her, slam his cock into her. When she came the second time, her body almost slid down into the water. Derek's hands held her up gently. She blinked twice.

"I'm tired." She shut the shower off drowsily and used a towel to get most of the moisture off of herself. When she was sure she had her legs back, she turned Derek off and stood there alone in the bathroom.

"No more box man for a bit." Meg yawned hugely and stumbled into bed. Her ebony hair fanned out on the pillow, and she pulled the comforter over herself.

* * * *

Ethan told himself to breathe. So he'd just virtually fucked his test subject. *So what?* All in the name of science. And the raging hard-on he'd had for days. Ever since he saw a smooth ass fill his computer screen. *God, she was beautiful.*

He shut his eyes and recalled every image. She was tall. His toy was well over six feet, but the woman came to

56

his shoulders. Full breasts. Pale, pink nipples. Hips that flared and curved. And shoulder-length jet-black hair. On her head and her pussy.

Her pussy.

Ethan could see every inch of it. He made his toy keep his eyes open as he sucked and licked her from top to bottom. His mouth actually watered. What he wouldn't give to be the one giving her every inch of his tongue and his cock.

It had to be unethical. *Fuck*. Ethan raked his hands through his short red hair. This is exactly what Colin would do. It wasn't right. She didn't know she was being watched. That wasn't part of the information she was given. Colin made sure of that. The terms were so wrapped up in legalese, she'd need a lawyer to figure them out.

The woman wouldn't be suspicious. As far as she knew, she'd been given a toy to pleasure herself and that's all. A couple of phone calls. Rate a toy. And she was done.

Except…

Ethan blew out a breath. Except she was on his mind all the time. He would rush to his computer to see if she was using the toy so he could watch. And this time, he had actually programmed words into the toy's mouth. *I like fucking you.* No lie there. The evidence was all over the cloth in his hand.

Ethan stood up and walked toward the shower. A little steam, and maybe he could think straight. Or at least with the right head. Ethan turned the shower on and threw his clothes in the hamper. He stepped beneath the spray and told himself to relax.

He moved his head around and was satisfied with the two short pops. Now if he could only make his shoulders loosen up.

The hot water beat down on him, and Ethan touched the cool tiles on the wall. The woman liked being pinned up against them. Her nipples touched the solid surface while being banged from behind.

His cock roused, and his hand moved down to stroke it. His left hand moved his cock up and down while his right cupped his balls. And she liked a mouth between her legs, sucking on her sweet pussy. Ethan threw back his head at the visual. He would lie on the bed, and she would straddle his face. Opening her pussy to his mouth. His hands would move up and cup her breasts while she rode his face, and he fucked her with his tongue. She tasted sweet. He would lick every inch of her and feel her clit swell against his tongue.

His stroke quickened. "Yes," Ethan cried out as he came. His cock jerked its release, and he tried to calm his frantically beating heart.

Virtually fucking her was unethical. But maybe he could work his way into her life. Ethan sighed. *Maybe.*

* * * *

Meg smiled over at her thirteen-year old student. Shannon was a quick study. She already had the basics down for social studies and science. But math and English kicked her ass. Right now, Shannon's pencil scratched across her paper as she tried to figure out the algebra problem.

"These letters suck," she announced.

Meg laughed and shook her head. "Maybe now, love. But it'll get easier."

"When?" Shannon demanded. She lifted her head and shook her black hair out of her face. "I'm sick of not knowing what I'm doing. Criminey! I'm behind everyone in my class." Her green eyes showed regret and embarrassment.

"Listen to me," Meg said firmly. "That is why you're gifted with my time. I happen to be a very good Algebrarian. Or something." She winked at Shannon's laugh. "And I won't let you fail. So buck up. Once you get it, you've got it."

"I'm never going to get it," Shannon moaned. "Never."

"And that positive attitude is doing wonders for you."

Shannon stuck out her tongue and then giggled.

Meg shook her finger at her. "Enough, young lady. Finish up today's work. Turn it in. I'll look over it, and we'll see what we need to work on next time." She waited while Shannon scribbled a couple of more answers and then ripped the paper out of the notebook.

Meg took the paper and set it on the desk. "Anything else?"

The teenager bit her lip and cocked her head to the side. "Are you still tutoring Danny?"

Ah, the beautiful dark-haired boy with a flair for football and little else. She noted the soft blush in her student's cheeks and hid her smile. Apparently, Shannon was interested in more than schooling today.

"Yes." Meg stood up and pulled her hair back into a ponytail. "I'll see him later this afternoon. Something you would like me to pass along?"

"You're teasing me." Shannon dropped her head.

"Only a little." Meg lifted the girl's head up gently. "I can see you like him. And having a crush on a good-looking boy is hardly something new. I've had a few crushes in my time, also."

"But they probably knew you were alive," she mumbled.

"I should have been so lucky." Meg sighed and sat on the edge of her desk. "I was a plain teenager, Shannon. And not much has changed now. I'm simply older, wiser, and more confident."

"He only dates cheerleaders." Shannon's eyes were dejected. The green softened somehow, as if in pain. "And I don't exactly fit into that mold."

"Oh, honey." Meg pulled the girl close and hugged her tight. "I know it hurts right now. But someday you'll find someone who doesn't care what your outsides look like. Just your insides." She tapped the girl's temple. "And how much algebra you know."

Shannon laughed and hugged her back. "Thanks, Meg."

"You're welcome, hon." She handed the teenager her algebra book and watched her tuck it inside her backpack. "I expect great things from you. Danny or no Danny."

"Yes, ma'am."

Meg escorted her to the door where she had one of her drivers take the girl home. She shut the door quietly behind her and stood in the foyer. A slow smile spread across her face. To be young and in "like" again. She chuckled. *How long ago it seemed.* Now she simply reverted to modern technology to scratch that itch. Her blue eyes shot upward toward her bedroom. *Derek.* Meg rolled the name around in her mouth before slowly uttering it aloud.

What would women of Shannon's generation have? More than a projection, with the way technology was going. Would she even have to worry about finding a man she liked? The thought unsettled Meg far more than she thought it would. Derek was harmless. A little distraction that took the place of plastic. *Right?*

She chewed on her bottom lip thoughtfully. *Is that all he was? Or a replacement? Would women in the future have little boxes of their own? Or would there be some type of "men catalog"?*

Meg shut the thought down with a sigh. It was all speculative. Here was where she resided. The present. She glanced at the expensive, gold watch on her wrist and smiled. Another ten minutes, and she would be graced by another student's presence. This one not nearly as affable as Shannon.

Brad was stubborn. Stubborn and headstrong. Meg sighed. The boy was being raised by his mother alone. And he had his bluff in on her already. Fourteen years old and already more of a man than his daddy had obviously been. Brad was an intelligent, angry young man. Brilliant. It was his self-discipline that needed some assistance.

Meg pulled her hair back again and smiled. Maybe some homemade chocolate chip cookies would help. She walked into her kitchen and scooped her hand into the cow cookie jar. It *mooed* low, and she chuckled.

She had just turned around when she heard the knock on the front door. Meg rushed down the hall and opened it with a smile.

Brad stood there with a perennial frown etched into his features.

"Hey." He walked inside and dropped his backpack low on his arm.

"Hey." Meg shut the door behind her. She resisted the urge to smooth down his unruly brown hair. Brad didn't like being touched. Period. And certainly not by his tutor.

"In the mood for a cookie?" Meg held the cobalt blue platter out and smiled.

"Sure." He shrugged and scooped a couple into his hand. He munched on one while he followed her into the library.

"I thought we would go over your science today. What do you think?"

"Whatever." His brown eyes were hard as he shrugged. "You're the teacher."

Meg cocked her head to the side. "Care to share?" Her blue eyes took in the shadows in his face. Something was bothering him. As hard as he tried to hide it, he couldn't.

"Nah."

"Bribe you with another cookie?" Meg plucked a cookie up and held it in front of her.

Brad looked up and met her eyes, searching. "Why do you like me?"

The simple question sounded as if it were ripped from his soul. The boy's pain was palpable in the room. She gathered herself for a minute.

"Because you're a smart young man. Caring." Meg met his eyes and tried to convey everything she needed to in words. "I'll have you know that I don't waste my time with students who don't have potential. And you, my dear," she pointed at him, "have it."

Brad looked away quickly. His chin trembled for a minute before he stilled it out of sheer willpower.

"Thanks." The word was softly spoken but full of gratitude.

"No problem, Mister." Meg waggled another cookie in front of her. "This one's for me. Now open that science book, and let's get to it."

* * * *

Meg watched the last of her students leave and shut the door quietly. She pulled her ponytail out and ran her fingers through her fine, black hair. It was a long day but productive. Now she had the entire weekend to herself. She rubbed her blue eyes tiredly and stifled a yawn.

It was only around six o'clock. She padded to the kitchen in her socks and opened the refrigerator. *Sad.* She shook her head. *Very, very sad. A jar of pickles. A bottle of ketchup. One lone egg.* It was amazing she had everything to make the cookies.

"Shit," Meg muttered. Her stomach growled impatiently, and she shut the door with a little more force than necessary. Too many cookies and not enough real food wore on her. An evening trip to the grocery store seemed to be in order.

She dragged herself upstairs and changed into blue jeans and a peach T-shirt. Shopping for groceries on a Friday evening was probably a poor life choice, but she didn't feel like ordering in.

Meg hopped into her small car and drove to the nearest grocery store. She let her mind wander over her day, examining every part. Her thoughts snagged on Brad and his question. It hit her hard, and she struggled to keep herself distant and not gather the boy to her. She hadn't lied in her answer. But how could she tell a fourteen-year-old boy how special he was without completely sounding like an idiot?

She pulled into the grocery store parking lot and killed the engine. Brad needed new shoes for one. The sight of his beat-up tennis shoes pulled at her heart. And Meg knew his mother wouldn't accept financial help at all. So she made a mental note to contact one of her people to find out where the woman shopped and offer a discount on shoes. He was also in dire need of a haircut, but that was more of a personal decision.

Meg sighed as she got out of the car and started toward the store. *Maybe some lunch meat. Bread. Soda.* Her mind was whirring along when she grabbed a grocery cart and cruised the aisles.

Necessities. Meg rounded the first corner and nearly laughed aloud. A man stood there, puzzled in front of the numerous cans of tomatoes. He would take one down, examine the label, and then put it back. She watched for about a minute and took the time to study the man.

Tall. Short, red hair. Her eyes traveled down his body. Muscular. Solid. Those hands that picked up the cans were large. Each can seemed to disappear in his grip. He would read each and every word on the can before he set it gently down.

Have mercy. He looked like he was conducting an experiment. *It was only tomatoes.*

"Problems?" she inquired mildly.

The man's head whipped around quickly and pinned her with clear, blue eyes. His jaw dropped quickly, and she watched him snap it shut with an effort.

Meg moved forward with a smile. "What exactly do you need the tomatoes for?" She picked up a can of diced tomatoes. "Salsa?" Then a can of tomato paste. "Sauce?"

The man cleared his throat a couple of times and pulled his red jacket tighter around himself. "Spaghetti sauce." His intent blue eyes never left her face while she talked.

"Then you'll be wanting these right here." Meg grabbed a couple of cans of tomato sauce and handed them to the man. His fingers reached out to grab them and brushed against her wrist.

The small shock made her jump, and she watched, amazed, as the man's eyes widened a fraction.

"Do I know you?" Meg asked.

"Not that I'm aware of." The man put the two cans in one of his hands and held out the other. "Ethan Fields."

She took his hand and liked the way her hand disappeared into his. *Strong man. And those eyes were simply beautiful.*

"Mr. Fields." She inclined her head with a smile.

"And you are?"

"Meg White." She looked down between them and noted their hands were still clasped. "May I have it back?"

"Sure." Ethan's smile spread slowly across his features. "I appreciate the help." He motioned to the cans in front of him. "It's a little confusing."

"No problem." Meg turned and started back toward the end of the aisle when his voice stopped her.

"Plans for dinner?"

She turned slowly and examined him closely. "We've only met, Mr. Fields."

"Please." His voice was steady and sincere. "I hate to eat alone."

"Are you cooking?"

"No." The word was flat and final. "Maybe some other time."

"Then I would be happy to. When and where?"

* * * *

Meg finished her shopping and unloaded her groceries back at her house. She threw the perishables in the refrigerator and told herself to calm down. *A simple dinner date. That's all it was.* She was worried for a second that he recognized her. But then his features smoothed out, and she let the worry go.

She hadn't thought twice about putting on a disguise. The publicity seekers were few and far between now. And for that, she was extremely grateful. Meg grimaced. Once upon a time, it was all she knew. Now there were bigger stories.

She checked the clock and hurried upstairs. Ethan asked her to meet him at seven thirty at his home. Meg opened her closet door and thumbed through outfits. Something nice. But casual. She didn't want him getting the wrong impression. *A simple date.* The words reverberated in her head. Then why was she acting like a schoolgirl?

Because she never picked up a man in a grocery store. Meg bit back a giggle. It was funny, actually. Erica would die from shock.

Her eyes lit upon the multi-colored scarf that covered up her toy. She bit her lip and thought about giving him a workout before she went, but somehow it didn't seem right. When she came home, she would pleasure herself. And all the pent-up desire in her would have a release.

Meg stayed in control. Always. There was too much at stake. Too much to lose to ever let that fragile peace in her life be disrupted. Yet here she stood, thumbing through her closet and worrying about making a good impression. On a man who couldn't pick out the right can of tomatoes at the store. Wonders never ceased.

* * * *

Ethan watched Meg leave the grocery parking lot and tried to gather himself to actually put the key into the ignition of his car. His hands shook slightly, and he cursed roundly. It didn't help that his cock still strained the confines of his blue jeans and had been since he spotted her. The object of his lust stood six feet away, looking entirely too desirable, and making conversation about cans of tomatoes.

It was surreal.

He gave up trying to fit the key in and simply sat there. Ethan brought back her image and bit back a groan.

The sable hair pulled back in a ponytail, accenting her aristocratic features. Bright, blue eyes sparkled with intelligence and humor. And her mouth. Ethan licked his suddenly dry lips. Her mouth called to him. The full, lower lip and perfectly bowed upper lip.

His mind's eye recalled she was wearing jeans and a T-shirt. Both accented her curves, and his hands itched to grab her hips and pull her tightly against him. Thank God he had a jacket on. It had served him well to shield his twitching cock.

And her scent. Ethan's hands clenched tightly on the steering wheel. It was a light scent. Floral. He pictured fields of flowers. And now he couldn't get any of his mental pictures out of his head.

They had a dinner date. What possessed him, he would never know. But he was going to have dinner with his test subject. *Shit.*

Colin would have his balls on a platter if he knew. All Ethan's talk of ethics. But ethics weren't the first thing that came to mind when he thought of Meg White. And Colin wouldn't ever have to know.

Shifty. All the subterfuge didn't set well with him. If he could keep his work and his personal life separate, there wouldn't be a problem anyway. Ethan glanced at the clock and started his car. He needed to drive home and order some Chinese takeout. And get ready for his date with a woman who already meant more to him than he cared to admit.

* * * *

Meg glanced down at the set of directions again with a frown. Ethan's handwriting was almost illegible at points. *Was that a right or a left?* She squinted her eyes as if that would magically make the letters easier to read. *Oh shit. It was neither.* He had written "north" down.

She sighed and shot her eyes upwards. *Why did men feel the need to use directions when left and right were universal?* Meg shook her head. She could get lost in a mall. This whole "north" thing was sure to make her late. Her compact car didn't have any of the bells and whistles. But her black SUV, which sat safely in her garage, had it all. Hell, it would damn near drive itself.

It was already dark outside, and she hit her hand on the steering wheel. There was no number on the piece of paper, so she couldn't call. The man was a bit absentminded. *Ethan*, she reminded herself. Maybe he was listed.

Meg hurriedly punched in information on her cell phone and waited for the disinterested voice to tell her his address. Thank God there was only one. Or she wouldn't make it to dinner at all.

Fifteen minutes later, Meg pulled into the driveway she hoped was the right one. She had been completely on the wrong side of town. And wasn't that a kick in the ass? She stepped out of her compact car and smoothed down her emerald pantsuit. The top was a little risqué. It only had three buttons that started right below the swell of her breasts. The pants hugged her hips and then flared down and belled at the bottom. Her green heels completed the picture nicely. Meg ran her fingers through her hair one last time as she looked at the house.

It was nice, she mused. One story but large. It was half-brick and painted a cream color on the rest. There had to be at least three bedrooms inside. The front had a window on either side of the door. The left, she surmised, would be the kitchen. And the right would be a bedroom. The slate roof sloped down and over large bay windows on the left side. The front lawn was manicured and showed signs of care. A light burned brightly on the porch, and she stepped up to it.

Meg tapped lightly and was rewarded a minute later with the man of the house. Once again, she felt that shiver of recognition, and told herself that she really was hard up. Be that as it may, she couldn't help but admire his ruggedly handsome face. His nose was a little off-kilter, and she found that endearing. Those beautiful blue eyes fixed on her, and she could have sworn her heart skipped a beat.

Nonsense. She wouldn't fall all over herself for the first real man who asked her out. That was sheer stupidity. And stupid, she wasn't.

"Come in." Ethan opened the door and swept his arm wide.

Meg nodded her thanks and stepped inside. She stopped in the foyer and waited for Ethan to show her where he wanted her. Her eyes flit across the furnishings in front of her, and she bit back a grin. Very masculine greens and browns melded in the living room where he started a fire. The flames licked up higher, and she was glad there was a chill in the air. She loved a fireplace.

"Please." Ethan grasped her elbow lightly and escorted her into the living room. "Have a seat."

Meg sank down onto the brown leather couch and tucked her purse beside her. She smiled up at Ethan and noted he looked particularly well put together. His white evening shirt was tucked into his tan khakis. The sleeves were rolled up to his elbows, and she noted the light red hair on his arms. She wanted to touch him and quickly dug her hands into the couch cushions. *Like hell.*

"Stay here." Ethan smiled down at her. "I've got everything under control."

She smiled up at him. "Do you?"

"Yes." He turned on his heel and walked back into the kitchen.

Meg watched him go and couldn't help but focus on the nice ass in those khakis as he walked away. She licked her lips and quickly told herself to snap out of the lust. *Dinner. A simple dinner.*

* * * *

Ethan walked calmly into the kitchen and stepped out of sight. His hands shook slightly as he tried to calm his breathing. *She was beautiful. So fucking beautiful.* And she was sitting on the couch in his living room in an outfit that made him want to tear it off her with his teeth.

The green material clung to her breasts, and he could see down her shirt when she sat down. That was a particularly welcome bonus. Her soft breasts swelled up, and his mouth watered at the sight. *Just a taste.* The minute the thought formed, he could feel his cock rising to the occasion. That's when he made himself scarce. The last thing he needed was to entertain his guest with a raging hard-on.

Ethan put the Chinese containers full of Hawaiian chicken, garlic chicken, and chow mein on the silver trays. And then finished the presentation with two wineglasses. The red wine chilled in the living room in the bucket.

Ethan took a deep breath and tried to calm his frantically beating heart. He wouldn't think of peeling Meg's clothes off and pleasuring her until she cried out his name. Over and over again. No. That wasn't on the menu. He would act civilized and make small talk. Get her to like him. Build a friendship.

He took one last calming breath, picked up the tray, and walked back into the living room.

Chapter 4

Meg found herself laughing at Ethan's stories and enjoying every minute of the dinner. She ate more than her share of Chinese food and drank a couple of glasses of red wine. She found out that they had a warped sense of humor in common, and that tickled her. When Meg asked about his job, there was a slight pause. And then he told her he was doing valuable research. He wouldn't expound any, but she didn't push. She understood and respected privacy.

She told him she was a tutor, and he asked about her students. Meg appreciated that. A lot of people would simply dismiss her tutoring as "busy work." But Ethan seemed genuinely interested. She found herself talking about Brad. Meg outlined the situation and asked Ethan his opinion.

"What are his grades like?"

"His science aptitude is off the chart." Meg took a sip of wine and shook her head. "But his discipline is iffy. And his teachers are tired of fighting with him. He has above average intelligence, but everything else is a struggle."

Ethan narrowed his eyes. The story sounded familiar. It was his. And the troubled student intrigued him. "Single parent family?"

"Yes." Meg cocked her head to the side and watched as Ethan's eyes grew dim. It was fascinating. "What are you thinking?" she murmured softly.

There was a minute of silence. And then, Ethan murmured, "I'd like to meet him."

"Why?"

Ethan chuckled softly. "He sounds a lot like me."

"You were a hellraiser?" Meg's eyebrows arched in disbelief. "You? With the tomato issues?"

"Hey!" His mouth stretched in a grin. "Cease and desist with the bashing, woman. I'm culinary ignorant."

She threw back her head and laughed. "Culinary ignorant?" she repeated when she caught her breath. "Oh Lord! That is too rich."

Ethan winked at her. "That's my above average intelligence showing." That sent her off into another gale of laughter.

Meg clutched her stomach as tears streamed down her face. "Please quit," she begged. "You're killing me."

He enjoyed watching her laugh. Sure, her breasts heaved, but he also liked the way her nose wrinkled. *Cute.* And then he made the mistake of touching her. Just a small touch to the tip of her nose.

Meg's laughter tapered off, and she studied him quietly. "My nose fascinates you?"

"It wrinkles when you laugh." Ethan's blue eyes studied hers intently. "I like it."

"Thanks." Her voice sounded breathless to her own ears. She told herself to breathe as he moved in closer. Those blue eyes still searched as his head dipped and his mouth brushed against hers. A simple graze of lips against lips. It was light. Fleeing. But it held a promise of things to come.

Meg moved back a little and looked directly into Ethan's eyes. She reached out and touched his lips softly. "You have a lovely mouth."

"That's my line." His voice was a husky timbre in the room.

She sighed and stood. "And I have to be going home."

"Because I kissed you?"

Meg turned and shook her head. "Because this is our first date. And I don't make a habit of making out with strangers."

Ethan stood also. "Fair enough. How about a second date? That might make me less strange."

She chuckled. "Don't be charming."

"I can't help myself. It goes with my above average intelligence." His blue eyes grinned down at her.

"If you have such an abundance of IQ, then why didn't you write simple directions to your house? I was clear across town before I dialed information and found you." Meg looked up at him and waited.

"I'm an idiot savant."

She rolled her eyes. "Clever."

Ethan smiled. "What are the odds of a second date?"

"Pretty good," Meg admitted. She picked up her purse and walked toward the front door. Ethan touched her arm lightly, and she turned around.

Time seemed to stop as he lowered his mouth to hers. And this time it wasn't a gentle brush of lips. It was hot and demanding.

His mouth slanted across hers with an intensity that left Meg clutching at his shoulders. Ethan's tongue moved in slow circles in her mouth. Teasing. Testing.

She groaned low in her throat as he stroked her tongue with his own. Then he sucked gently on her lips while tracing every inch with his tongue. Meg responded with a passion that shocked her. Gone was all rationale. She wanted more. And she wanted it now.

Ethan's hand moved down to her shirt, and Meg felt a button pop open. And then another. And when he moved his mouth away from hers, she nearly begged him not to quit. But then his mouth sank lower. He brushed his lips against the soft flesh of her breast, and her nipples tightened in arousal.

"Please," she murmured. Meg's hands clutched tightly in Ethan's hair. His breath moved across her skin until she felt his tongue lap gently at her nipple. Her back arched further.

"Yes," she breathed out in a sigh. Ethan flicked his tongue back and forth against the bud. Her body shook helplessly in arousal. And then he took it fully into his mouth and sucked it slowly.

His other hand trailed down her body and fitted her ass in his hand. Ethan brought her body tighter against his as he pleasured her nipple. He lifted his head and started to move to the other one when Meg's trembling hand stopped him.

"Ethan." The word was soft but forceful.

He looked up with hazy blue eyes full of desire. Meg moved back a step and buttoned her shirt back up. She bit her lip and met his eyes.

"I think I let that get out of hand. I'm sorry." Her eyes pleaded with his to understand.

Ethan took a minute to collect himself. But even half an hour wouldn't cool his blood at this minute. Meg's taste was in his mouth, and he wanted more. Craved it. And he didn't understand why she halted what they were doing. *Didn't a woman who was so sexual welcome it?*

"I think I need to go."

He moved closer and tried not to grimace at the pain in his balls. "Meg. I'm sorry. It's my fault. I guess I thought a simple goodnight kiss wasn't enough. I didn't mean to push."

She tried to smile. "Goodnight, Ethan."

He watched her walk down the driveway and leave. Ethan hit the doorframe with all his might and winced at the pain that shot through his hand. It didn't lessen the pain in his crotch, but it did reroute it.

"Smooth." He shook his head and slammed the front door. "No wonder I don't get out of the lab much. I'm a fucking dating disaster."

* * * *

Meg leisurely drove home. Her body was still uncomfortably aware of how much she wanted to have sex. She was still wet and needed satisfaction. *Derek. You and I have plans.*

She parked in her driveway and opened her front door. The house was quiet. But for once it wasn't comforting. It was overwhelming. She hung her keys on the peg and shut the door behind her. There was the low hum of the appliances, but that was it.

"I like it quiet," she reminded herself aloud. "Quiet is good. Being alone means I can do whatever I want. Whenever I want." The reasoning sounded like a petulant child, and she frowned.

Fuck it. Meg walked upstairs and kicked off her shoes in her bedroom. The multi-colored scarf covered up her good time. She plucked it up gently and laid it next to the black box. She flicked the switch and was instantly rewarded.

Derek stood before her with the blond hair and blue eyes of most of her masturbatory fantasies. His body was muscular and perfect. He wore the same jeans and T-shirt he always appeared in. And Meg was mesmerized.

"What would you like?" His blue eyes held a promise of one hell of a night.

"Undress me," she commanded.

He moved forward and stopped a mere foot from her. His sure hands moved to unbutton her green blouse. One button. Two buttons. Derek moved to the third button when Meg's hands stopped him.

"Kiss me."

He moved forward and took her mouth with his.

The kiss was executed perfectly, but it left Meg wanting. She lifted her head and looked into his light blue eyes. "Make me want you."

"I don't understand."

His softly spoken words irritated her.

"Never mind," she muttered. "Just fuck me."

Meg felt herself moved to the bed and laid down. The last button on her shirt popped open, and Derek shifted his mouth to take her breast into his hot mouth. She moaned and clutched the back of his head. But it wasn't blonde hair she wanted to clutch. It was light red hair. The thought irritated her.

She told herself she was being stupid. And then she simply blocked it all out as the desire slammed through her. "Yes," she moaned. "Yes."

Derek's hands cupped her breasts together as his mouth brought one nipple into his mouth and then the other. One hand wandered down to the waistband of her green dress pants and slipped inside. Fingers plucked at the elastic of her panties and probed gently downwards.

Meg spread her legs further at the feel of Derek's fingers touching her pussy lips. He stroked gently while his mouth sucked relentlessly on her nipples. She arched her hips up to meet his questing fingers and moved hers down to show him exactly where she wanted them. But as soon as the thought formed, he moved two fingers deep inside of her.

She cried out in pleasure as his tongue formed a trail down her body. Derek slid her pants and panties down off her ass and past her legs.

And then his mouth replaced his fingers. Meg put her legs over Derek's shoulders and gripped his hair tightly in her hand. His tongue worked expertly on her swollen clit, and she writhed under its ministrations.

The first orgasm jerked her entire body up, and she ached with pleasure. Her body convulsed rapidly, and she trembled. "More," she begged.

Derek moved her legs down gently and spread them apart. He stroked her labia softly and moved on top of her. Meg shifted to accommodate him and moaned as he slid his hard cock into her. She wrapped her legs tightly around him and shuddered as his sure strokes brought her closer and closer to another climax.

Meg arched her body up and cried out as another orgasm ripped through her. Derek slid off of her and lay on his side next to her. As his fingers trailed over her bare body, she turned to face him.

"What happens when I turn you off?"

"I cease to exist." His words were spoken matter-of-factly.

She frowned, and her blue eyes darkened. "Does it bother you? The fact you're not real?"

"No." Derek took her hand and kissed her fingertips. "This is my purpose. And I understand that." He tilted his head to the side. "You need not feel sorry for me."

Meg shrugged. "I don't."

He lifted her chin with his hand and looked into her eyes. "You do."

"Look." She propped herself up on her elbow and studied the man in front of her. "I understand you're a device. A toy. A tool. I get that. But the fact that you're so lifelike is sometimes disturbing."

"Why?" His eyes were puzzled.

Meg shook her head. "You're like a genie in a bottle. I pop the cork and get my wish." She smiled softly. "Which has its advantages. I was simply trying to understand." She stood up and walked over to the black box. "Goodnight, Derek."

"Goodnight, Meg."

Her hand flicked the switch, and he disappeared.

* * * *

Ethan turned off his computer and stared into the darkness of his room. He loved to watch Meg come. It was almost an addiction. And when she left his house, he prayed she would switch on the toy and use it for her leisure. He wasn't disappointed.

Meg's breasts spilled out of her top, and he groaned as the toy took them into his mouth. And when the toy slid his fingers into her, Ethan drove himself crazy thinking of the feel of her. Hot, wet, and willing.

His cock still throbbed painfully below the desk. Ethan swore he wouldn't use the data to get himself off, but now he was paying the price. He pushed back from the desk and hobbled into his bedroom. A hot shower should do the trick.

Ethan stripped his clothes off and started the shower. He left the water almost unbearably hot and stepped underneath it. His body tightened immediately, and he groaned. As long as he wasn't watching her while playing with himself, it wasn't unethical, was it?

His right hand grasped his hard cock in his hand and moved it slowly up and down.

* * * *

"Wake up, man!"

Ethan blinked hazily and tried to focus on the annoying voice in his office. "What?" he growled.

Colin frowned and looked down at his friend. "You look like shit." He sat down on the edge of Ethan's desk and peered closely at his friend. "Been getting any sleep?"

"Loads."

"Right." Colin picked up a piece of paper and scanned the information. "You're a little sucked up in this whole project, don't you think?"

Ethan snatched the paper from his hands and snarled. "I'm doing research, Colin. Get off my ass."

"I wasn't on your ass. Yet. But I'm about to be." Colin's brown eyes took in the disheveled and raggedy appearance of his right-hand man. "You're taking the day off."

"No." The word fell flat in the quiet room.

"Yes."

"Fuck off." Ethan gathered the loose sheets of paper and stacked them neatly around his desk. "I'm busy here."

"What's going on?" Colin studied Ethan. "I've seen you become absorbed in other studies. But nothing like this. And I'd like to know why."

"This could make our careers."

"So?" Colin stood up and looked around. "You need a break. Take it."

Ethan opened his mouth again, but Colin held up his hand. "Now." Colin walked out and shut the door behind him.

"Son of a bitch." Ethan slammed his hand down on the desk. "Bossy bastard." He stood and snatched his keys off the hook by the door. If he didn't take the break now, Colin would be back in five minutes. And then five minutes after that. He wouldn't get a damn thing done. Better to take a brief break and then back to business.

* * * *

Meg planned her studies with her students and rubbed her eyes blearily. She hadn't slept for shit last night, and right now she was dragging. Thoughts of Ethan filtered through her head until past two o'clock in the morning, and she resented it. Hell, she didn't even know the man. What was he doing in her thoughts?

She gathered her notes and filed them in their folders. Tomorrow was going to be busy with three different students. Brad would be one of them. Meg bit her lip. She wanted to call Ethan. She didn't want to call Ethan. *When did one man who couldn't even pick out his own tomatoes become such a pain?*

Brad needed a male figure in his life he could talk to. His mother worked her ass off just to give him the basics. His father had been absent his entire life. And as much as Meg could do for him with his education, she didn't know shit about teenage males. Hell, she had problems with adult males, too.

She made up her mind quickly and called Ethan's house. Meg wrapped her fingers through the phone cord and told herself to quit acting like such an idiot.

"Hello?"

Ethan's voice was impatient and edgy.

"Hello." Meg prayed for guidance. "I was hoping to leave a message."

"Meg?" His tone softened perceptibly. "I thought you were my idiot boss. Sorry."

"Quite all right." She took a deep breath. "Do you have plans tomorrow?"

"No."

She ran her tongue over her teeth. "Would you perhaps come over to my house and meet with Brad? Maybe give him a little direction? Male guidance?"

Ethan chuckled. "I'd be glad to. About what time?"

Meg gave him directions to her house and the time Brad was supposed to be there. "I'd like to return the favor. Would you care to stay for dinner?"

"I'd love to."

She grinned at the phone. "Splendid. I'll expect you tomorrow around three. Goodbye."

"Bye, Meg."

She hung up the phone and did a little dance. *So far, so good.* Now if she could just resist fucking his brains out, she'd be great. Meg pulled her hair back and rubbed her forehead. She would not make some stupid ass mistake by sleeping with the first man she was attracted to. Those things never worked out. There would be cursing and accusations. And she liked Ethan. So sleeping with him was a very bad idea.

"Very bad," she muttered. Then why couldn't she get it out of her head?

* * * *

Meg changed clothes three times the next morning before she decided on a simple pair of blue jeans and a creamy yellow blouse. She made sure she had food for the students and plenty of soda. She allowed them two cans per study session. One during and one for the road.

Her stomach clenched at the thought of Ethan being in her house. "I'm overreacting," she muttered. "Everything will be fine. We won't kiss. Hold hands. Nothing. Just friends." Meg thought of the black box upstairs. "I already have something to scratch my itch."

She blew out a breath when she heard the doorbell. Her first student arrived.

Meg spent the next couple hours educating teenage girls about the importance of math and science. Neither was too impressed. She tried not to lose her patience as the second one was more inclined to worry about whether her bangs were straight or not. Which was why she had a very low "C" in two of her core curriculum classes.

"Melanie." Meg put her hand down on the table by the girl's book. "You know how to do this. You know how important this is. Why do you keep acting like it doesn't matter?"

The teenage girl's baby blue eyes didn't move up from the book in front of her. She shook her head. "I don't understand any of it."

Meg pulled papers out from a folder that the science teacher sent her. "How can you be making exactly a seventy in two classes? But on the tests, you manage to get one problem correct and the same type problem wrong? I don't understand."

Melanie's eyes widened in shock. Meg tapped the book impatiently. "You don't need these sessions, do you?"

"Don't be mad!" The girl looked up with pleading eyes. She bit her lip. "I may know a little more than my tests show."

"A little?" Meg shook her head.

"Fine." The girl blew out her breath in a rush. "A lot. I'm capable of straight A's." She looked at Meg defiantly. "Are you going to tell my father?"

"Could you please explain to me why you would go to so much trouble to sabotage your grades? I know I'm lovely company, but this is ridiculous."

Melanie chuckled. "You're not bad." She looked down at her book again. "But it's more about my boyfriend."

"Ah." The word was short and knowing. Meg sat down across from the girl.

"He's not very smart." The words came out quickly. "And he doesn't like a girlfriend who's smarter than he is."

Meg nodded. "So you're willing to sacrifice one afternoon a week for this stellar specimen of adolescent maleness. I see."

"I knew you wouldn't understand," the girl muttered.

"You're right. I don't." Meg shrugged. "I assume you two are planning to go to college together, if he decides to go. And you're also going to work at the same office. And during this whole relationship, you'll be willing to make yourself less so he can feel good about himself?"

"He's a great guy!" Melanie protested.

"What about him is so great?" Meg waited patiently.

"He makes me laugh. And he cares about me."

"So. You're willing to dumb yourself down for the greater relationship good?" Meg shook her head. "If he cares about you, he would be happy for you. Whether your grades were higher or not. He should be proud." She brought Melanie's head up so she could look her student in the eye. "Don't settle for less than you are."

The timer went off, and Meg glanced up at it. She sighed. "I suppose I'll see you next week."

"I suppose." The girl gathered her books and put them in her backpack. She walked slowly to the door and out to her car.

Meg wanted to say something else, but she didn't know what. Being a teenager was hard enough in today's world without the compounding of relationship woes. She made sure Melanie was safely on her way before she shut the door.

"Shit." She sighed. Meg walked slowly back into the study and tidied up a bit. She plucked the books she needed from her shelf and put them on the large oak desk. Then she walked into the kitchen to make sure she had snacks and sodas. That was one thing she was certain Brad would like. He was a growing boy, or so he liked to inform her. And she had some great snacks.

Meg pulled her hair back again and tried to calm her nervous stomach. She checked the refrigerator and made sure all her ingredients for dinner were in there. Then she popped the top of a diet soda and leaned back against her kitchen sink.

"I am a grown woman. I am capable of acting like an adult." She repeated the mantra three more times before the doorbell rang. Her hand shook slightly as she placed the can back on the cabinet and walked to the front door.

Meg opened the door quickly and stepped back. Ethan smiled down at her. His red hair was slightly tousled from the wind. And his cheeks were rosy.

"Nice place," he commented, while he walked inside.

"Thanks." She smiled and took his dark blue jacket. "Can I get you anything?"

"Perhaps a bit of caffeine?"

She nodded her head toward the kitchen. "Follow me." Meg was extremely conscious of the large man behind her and tried to act as naturally as possible. She stepped into the kitchen and opened a cabinet by the cream-colored refrigerator.

"Would you like a glass?" Meg turned just in time to see him studying her ass. She bit her lip and turned back around.

"No. A can is fine."

She licked her lips and walked over to the refrigerator and took out a can. "Here you go."

Ethan immediately opened it and drank half of it in one serious gulp.

Meg's eyes widened.

He brought the can back down and grimaced. "Listen. About the other night…"

She held up her hand. "Don't."

Ethan took her hand in his large one and pulled it down. "I'm sorry."

She sighed and shook her head. "I'm sorry, too."

"We're two sorry individuals, aren't we?" Ethan's blue eyes shone with laughter.

"Seems like it." Meg rolled her eyes. "I'm out of practice with dating." She looked up at Ethan apologetically. "I don't get out much. I'm rather inept at this."

He blinked at looked down at her. "You're kidding, right?"

Meg shook her head.

"I'm a workaholic," he admitted. "My job means a lot to me. I have tunnel vision." He glanced at Meg. "Had tunnel vision. Until a lovely woman rescued me from certain tomato disaster."

"The least I could do." She grinned.

Ethan brought her hand up and kissed the back of it. "Let's show your student the light, and then we'll discuss this more over dinner. How's that?"

Meg smiled softly. "That's good." She opened her mouth to say something else when the doorbell rang. "Come on." She motioned to Ethan. "Sounds like Brad's arrived."

* * * *

Ethan watched the angry adolescent's face as he took in the sight of Brad. *Immediately territorial.* The boy wanted to protect Meg.

"Who's this guy?" Brad jerked his thumb toward Ethan. "He a little slow, too?"

"Brad." Meg sighed and shook her head. "Ethan is a friend of mine. A brilliant scientist, or so he says." She motioned to the two males. "Come on. I have refreshments in the study."

Brad glanced warily at Ethan and followed Meg.

Ethan gave them both a little space and watched the interaction. Brad liked Meg, that was certain. The boy would look at her when she wasn't looking at him. And as soon as she did, he etched that scowl on his face. He was also pleased when she brought out the snacks and soda. But what surprised Ethan was the look on the teenager's face when Meg brought out the books. Brad appeared almost reverent.

Meg brought out a notebook and looked at it. "We seem to be ready to move onto chemistry." She glanced at Ethan. "Care to join us?"

"Sure." He sat a bit away from the boy and motioned to the books in front of him. "Do you know what a chemical equation is?"

"Sure." The boy rolled his eyes and looked at Meg.

Ethan bit back a smile. "Know how to balance one?"

Brad narrowed his eyes and looked at Ethan. "No."

Ethan took one of the notebooks and a pen out of his pocket. He started with a simple equation and turned it around to Brad. "You will."

Meg eased away from the table where the two males had their heads side by side. Ethan would point something out, and Brad would nod in agreement. And then Brad would write something down.

She quickly made her way to the kitchen, got herself another soda, and studied the clock on the wall. Seemed like her new brilliant friend was just what the doctor ordered for one surly teenager. Meg cocked her head to the side. Hard to imagine Ethan as some unruly teenager with an attitude. He seemed almost introverted and cautious now.

Except when his mouth was on her body. Meg bit back her groan and looked around for something to occupy her remaining minutes. The last thing she needed was to remember his hands and mouth where they shouldn't have been.

"Friends," she muttered. Meg opened the refrigerator and took out a couple of steaks. She stepped out onto her back porch and studied the sky. *Nice evening for grilling.* She walked back into the kitchen and quickly wrapped four potatoes and four ears of corn. Ethan was a big man. No doubt he had a big appetite.

"A really big appetite." Meg sighed and put the aluminum foil up. "I need professional help."

"We're done."

She whirled around and saw the two males grinning at her from the doorway. Meg smiled back. "I see. And no bloodshed. Red letter day, gentleman." She pulled a soda out and handed it to Brad. "One for the road."

"Thanks." He opened it and took a drink. "Ethan said I could keep a couple of his books here. Do you mind?"

"Of course not." Meg winked at him. "More work for you. Leave them in the library."

Brad looked up at the clock. "Gotta go." He glanced up at Ethan with a grin. "Later, man."

"Later." Ethan watched the teenager walk away.

Meg held up her hand. "Hold on a second. I have to make sure he makes it to the car." She walked to the front door and waved as Brad got into his mother's old car, and they drove off.

"Quite the mother hen, aren't you?"

She turned around and studied him. "Yes. It may seem unnecessary, but I think they like it. Not that they'll ever admit it." Meg shrugged sheepishly. "Plus, I like it." She shut the door and walked to the kitchen. "I think it's a nice gesture to see someone off."

"It is." Ethan fought back a grin.

"Quit smirking." Meg motioned to the back porch. "Can you handle a grill?"

His blue eyes crinkled in laughter. "You're kidding, right?"

Meg put her hands on her hips. "Does it look like I'm joking?"

"No. And that's what's funny." Ethan assumed a lengthened stance and motioned with his hand. "Give me the grilling tools, woman."

She snickered and turned to grab them out of the drawer. Meg put them in his outstretched hand and bowed low. "The cow awaits your attention."

Ethan threw back his head and laughed. "Cut like steaks, I hope."

"Sure." Meg motioned to the refrigerator. "But I also wrapped potatoes and corn." She opened the door. "How about a beer?"

"Love one." Ethan took it from her hand and accidentally brushed her fingers. He made a concerted effort to keep his eyes above her neck.

"We're playing with fire," Meg muttered.

"I thought you had propane."

She looked up at him with exasperation in every feature. "I'm not referring to the grill."

"Ah." Ethan took a long draw from the bottle and put it on the kitchen cabinet. "And what's so wrong with that?"

"Relationships are complicated." Meg brought out a beer for herself and kept her hands busy with it. "There are things you have to tell each other. Allowances to make. It's a lot of work."

He smiled. "So I've heard."

"Go ahead. Laugh." Meg brushed her ebony hair back and looked him square in the eye. "Aren't there things that you would rather keep to yourself?"

His smile faded quickly as thoughts of his research crept to the forefront of his mind.

"See?" Meg twisted the cap off and took a drink. "We need to remain friends. That's it. No pressure. No promises."

Ethan sighed. "Already have this all figured out, don't you?"

She shrugged.

He put down the tools and walked very slowly toward her. Meg's eyes grew large, and she opened her mouth, as if to tell him something. But Ethan wouldn't be denied. He put his finger against her lips and then quickly replaced it with his mouth.

Meg's head fell back, and she wound her arms around Ethan's neck. Desire slammed through her with a fierceness that scared the hell out of her. His mouth felt so good against hers. His tongue stroking hers. And then his hands moved down to cup her breasts, and she moaned deep in her throat.

Those large hands palmed both breasts, and heat shot through her body with a vengeance.

She wanted to grab Ethan's hair and bring his mouth down to her breasts. Put her nipple into his mouth and arch her body into him.

"Jesus." Meg struggled in his arms and tried to break contact.

Ethan moved back and dropped his hands to her waist. His blue eyes were hazy with desire. He licked his lips and looked down at her mouth. "I have food to cook." He stepped back without another word and walked outside.

"Too much. Too soon." Meg smoothed her shirt down and told herself to calm down. Why did she invite him over tonight? Not just for Brad. For herself. "Shit," she muttered. "I like him." *And wasn't that a bundle of complications?*

Chapter 5

When Meg was sure she wouldn't jump Ethan's bones, she walked outside to the patio. The white wrought iron patio furniture complemented the dark wood deck perfectly. Her mother picked out the pieces. And when they aged, Meg always replaced them with perfect replicas.

The large black grill gave off an aroma that made Meg's mouth water. Ethan expertly checked the food and winked at her.

Meg wrapped her arms around herself and moved closer to the grill. There was a slight nip in the air this evening, and she hadn't thought to bring out a jacket. Ethan moved toward her and rubbed her bare arms. Her lips twitched as his ministrations brought out more goosebumps. Just not the cold kind.

She stepped back and motioned to the grill. "If you can grill, why are you worried about tomatoes?"

Ethan shrugged. "Nice to be well-rounded. Throw some pasta together. Make some homemade sauce."

"Ah."

He gestured toward the large, rolling hills behind her house. "You've got quite a view here."

"Yes." Meg's voice was melancholy.

Ethan's eyes sharpened. "But it pains you."

"A bit." Her blue eyes gazed out in the dusk. "Sometimes the past is a hard mistress."

The statement intrigued Ethan, but he didn't question her. Maybe Meg was right. The secrets he kept could certainly destroy any chance of a relationship with her. And how would he break it to her that he watched her get freaky with a projection?

"What's wrong?" Meg watched Ethan's face in fascination. There was remorse. Chagrin. And then a rather large grimace. His thoughts clearly pained him.

"Nothing." He smiled briefly and turned back toward the grill. Ethan expertly flipped the steaks and took a drink of his beer. When he turned back around, Meg sat in one of the white chairs. She had her legs tucked up beside her and watched him carefully.

"What do you think of Brad?"

Ethan chuckled. "The kid's a handful. But you're right. He's intelligent. Now if we can just get him to believe that, we'll be halfway there." He tilted his head to the side. "Have you always wanted to teach?"

"Not always." Meg took a sip of beer. "But I've found that it calls to me. And who am I to ignore that?"

He took the corn and potatoes off and placed them in bowls. Then he turned to the steaks and sprinkled some spices on them.

Meg tilted her head back and closed her eyes. She could almost pretend this was her life. It had been too long between lovers. Too long between feeling as though she wanted to share a part of herself. She opened her eyes lazily and watched Ethan take the steaks off the grill. His large hands moved precisely and confidently. The same way they had moved over her bare skin.

"Penny for your thoughts."

Meg's eyes shot up to see Ethan staring down at her. "Inflation, my good man. My thoughts are pricey."

His blue eyes moved slowly over her face. "Do tell." Ethan set the food down and shut the grill's lid. Then he walked slowly over to Meg and knelt in front of her.

Her eyes softened as they traced over his features. He wasn't traditionally handsome. More like an overgrown boy in a man's body. And what a body. Meg reached out tentatively and ran her fingers through his short red hair. It was surprisingly soft, and she kept her hand there.

Ethan turned his head and placed a kiss lightly on her palm. Meg's breath caught in her throat. And then he traced his tongue over the center of her hand. Her left hand clenched in her lap before coming up and cupping the other side of his head.

He moved forward then between her legs. Meg moved her legs and wrapped them around his upper body.

Her pussy throbbed with need as Ethan ravaged her mouth with his own. And then those brilliant hands moved down to her shirt and lifted it up to give him access. Meg arched her back and moaned as his pulled her bra down over one breast and tugged on her nipple. Need shot through her, and she pulled on his hair, wanting more.

Ethan moved his mouth from hers and pushed her shirt up higher. He looked into Meg's face before he lowered his mouth to take her nipple with his tongue. His left hand moved over her left breast but didn't attempt to free it as he had her right.

"Please," she murmured.

He lifted his head. "Show me," he whispered.

Meg moved her hand up her stomach, to the bottom of her breast. She kept eye contact with Ethan the entire time. Then she gently slid the white fabric down, baring her breast to him. Meg brought his head closer and rubbed her hardened nipple against his lips. She watched Ethan flick his tongue back and forth against the nub. And the ache in her pussy grew until she was sure she was about to come all over herself.

Meg shifted slightly to allow herself room to rub her clit against Ethan's hard chest. Her pants became the enemy, and she growled low.

Ethan brought his head up, and Meg could see desire written clearly across his features. The evidence of his desire pressed up against her ankles, and she knew she wasn't the only one uncomfortably wet.

"Ethan." Meg licked her lips and tried to form a thought. He looked at her expectantly before he lowered his mouth to her breast again.

Meg felt something vibrate against the inside of her thigh and frowned. He was good, but he wasn't that good. *Did he have a vibrator in his pocket?* She tapped Ethan on the top of his head and waited.

"Huh?" He blinked.

"You're vibrating."

His pocket moved again, and he cursed roundly.

"Someone wants to get a hold of you," Meg tried to tease.

"I wanted you to get a hold of me." Ethan stood abruptly and yanked the phone out of his pocket. "What?"

Meg bit back a smile at his terse tone.

"You pick the worst fucking times to think you need me. Couldn't this wait until morning?" Ethan's eyes wandered over the wanton picture Meg made. She made no effort to cover herself.

She heard Ethan growl low. "Well, fuck you, too." He snapped the phone shut. He seemed to remember where he was and smiled apologetically. "Sorry."

Meg tucked herself back in her bra and lowered her shirt. Her panties were still wet, and she felt as if she were on the verge of orgasm. But she knew it was probably a better thing that Ethan had to leave.

"What's wrong?"

"My idiot boss." Ethan raked his fingers through his hair. "First he kicks me out of the office and now he can't live without me."

"Why do you put up with him?" Meg licked her lips and reached for her beer.

"He's also my best friend."

She covered her mouth to prevent spitting the beer out. The sentence dripped with disgust.

"Those pesky best friends." Meg wiped her mouth. "I feel your pain." She stood and shook her head. "I'll make you a plate."

Though still obviously attracted to each other, Meg felt the urge to fuck Ethan's brains out pass. She would go upstairs and wear herself out with Derek.

Ethan brought in all the tools and plates of food. He glanced at the clock and grimaced. "Not quite the all-nighter I had planned."

Meg moved toward him and brushed her lips softly against his. "There'll be other dinners. And maybe, if you're a good boy, you can have dessert, too."

Ethan slid his hands between their bodies and stroked the back of his knuckles against the tight vee of her pants. She fought the urge to rub up against him and purr like a kitten.

"There is something I have a taste for." His blue eyes darkened.

"Go." Meg stepped back and grabbed the plate from the kitchen table. "You've got to work. And I need to take a cold shower."

"Raincheck?"

Meg realized he was referring to more than just dinner, and she slowly smiled. "Yes."

Ethan cupped her head with his other hand and brought her lips to his. His tongue traced every curve and sucked gently on her bottom lip. "I love rainchecks."

* * * *

Meg watched Ethan pull away and blew out a shaky breath. She rested her head against the doorframe and wondered briefly if she had lost her mind. She didn't know Ethan. Of course, he was extremely intelligent and could grill one hell of a steak. Add to that the fact he made her want him with a mere touch.

"Shit." She shut the door and padded back into the kitchen. Her food looked unappetizing compared to what she wanted. Meg quickly wrapped the food and put it in the refrigerator. Her body didn't need sustenance right now. It needed sex.

Meg stripped off every vestige of clothing and walked upstairs to her bedroom. Normally, if she were this aroused, she would simply open her toy closet and work her way through her stock until she couldn't come anymore.

Thankfully, she now had the ultimate sex toy at her beck and call.

She would take a shower later. Right now she needed the pleasure of a man's hands on her body.

Meg reached out and put the earrings carefully in her ears. Then she switched the box on and all but purred at the sight of Derek.

"Nude," she commanded.

Derek stood there as naked as she. Meg held out her hand and smiled as Derek slid his into hers.

"You're aroused." Derek looked down into Meg's eyes.

"Yes." Meg sank to the bed and sat on the edge. She spread her legs wide and dipped one finger into her slippery slit. Derek sank to his knees and opened his mouth. She slid her finger inside and moaned as he sucked on the digit relentlessly.

Then his hands moved and cupped her ass. Derek brought her to the edge of the bed and smiled. His head dropped down until she could feel his breath on her wet pussy. Meg spread her legs as far as possible and waited for the first touch of his tongue against her silky skin.

The first stroke of that soft but firm tongue against her soaking pussy made her throw her head back and clutch the covers in her hand. Her nipples puckered, and she moaned. But she underestimated Derek. He didn't simply dive right in and bring her to orgasm. His hands that still gripped her ass worked her pussy against his questing tongue.

He fucked her smoothly, unerringly finding the nub that he knew would bring her pleasure.

Meg clutched his hair beneath her hand and tried to surge up, but he didn't let her. "Derek," she rasped. "Make me come."

He worked her ass off the bed in an easy motion that made her tremble with excitement. Soon her legs were hung over his shoulders while he ate her relentlessly.

"Yes," she cried out as the pressure in her body increased with every stroke of his tongue. "I want to come in your mouth." Meg shuddered as his strokes brought her closer and closer. She arched up hard and cried out at the force of the orgasm that flooded her body. She jerked up over and over again as the orgasm went on and on. Derek never lifted his head.

Meg collapsed weakly on the bed but didn't even have a chance to catch her breath before Derek's cock filled her. And the rhythm of his tongue was quickly replaced by the pounding of his cock in her pussy and his balls slapping against her ass.

She trembled at the impossible feeling of another orgasm building up. Her body arched up, and Meg cried out as the pleasure ripped through her.

Derek lowered her slowly to the bed and lay down beside her. Meg opened one eye and peered blearily at him.

"You're quite honestly the best sex toy I've ever come across. A new category. Five moans. Hands down."

"Thank you."

Meg chuckled. "No. Thank you." She maneuvered herself to the edge of the bed and flipped the switch on the black box. Then she took the earrings out of her ears. Her body sated for now. But she couldn't help but wonder about Ethan. How many moans could he give her?

She shivered in the cool air and pulled the covers over her shoulder. *Ethan.* Meg smiled as she drifted off to sleep. *That's what rainchecks were for.*

* * * *

Ethan slammed his car into park and sat in the parking lot, steaming. *Damn Colin! His timing couldn't have been worse.* The feel of Meg's skin against his mouth and hands was enough to make him hard while he sat there. He growled low and quickly stepped out of his car. He slammed the door shut and went inside the building. It had better be important.

Colin waited for him in the hallway to their offices. He smiled when he saw Ethan. "Get enough rest?"

"No." The word was short and irritable.

Colin's eyes narrowed. "Did I take you away from something," he wriggled his eyebrows, "promising?"

"Asshole." Ethan nodded. "Yes. So you better be dying up here or in dire need of my help. Because if you're not, we're done."

Colin smoothed back his dark hair. "Okay. Listen before you start yelling."

Dread climbed into Ethan's midsection and stayed there. "What have you done?"

"I pulled up numbers from the test subject. You seemed to have most of those. So I decided to dig a little deeper."

"Did you view the tapes?" Ethan struggled to keep his voice even and with the insane jealousy tearing at his guts.

"Don't be stupid." Colin shook his head. "You already threatened to put my nuts in a vice. I think complete objectivity is the way to go on this one."

"Complete objectivity," Ethan repeated blankly.

"Sure. That way there aren't any complications. Anyway." Colin started walking toward the lab, and Ethan followed him. "We've got bigger problems." He opened the door and motioned to the desk with reams of paper scattered across the top.

Ethan briefly thought about yelling at Colin to not eat his dinner in the lab but quickly dismissed the idea. The smell of a roast beef sub was beginning to make him nauseous. He swallowed convulsively and turned a fan on.

"What did you find?"

Colin spread the papers out and pointed at the spikes on the graphs. "Our toy seems to be experiencing numbers off the chart. I thought he had a baseline and didn't deviate from it."

Ethan frowned and thumbed through at least a dozen papers before lifting his head. His blue eyes were wide with shock. "This isn't possible."

"That's what I thought." Colin pulled up a screen and tapped out a few commands. Numbers scrolled past with amazing speed until he clicked on the charts. He printed out at least six more sheets and handed them to Ethan. "These are from tonight."

"Tonight?" Ethan's hands clenched tightly on the papers. He was scared shitless to look down on them but forced himself. *Impossible. It was utterly fucking impossible.* But page after page showed the hard proof. The toy was beginning to have emotions.

* * * *

Meg woke up late Saturday morning and stretched. Her body felt loose and limber from the previous night's sex. It wasn't making love. Not when there was an on/off button in play. And if she couldn't have Ethan next to her, Derek was awfully fun to play with. She yawned and lay there. Maybe Ethan would call today. She grinned and tapped the pillow next to her. *Wouldn't that be nice?*

Too soon? The irritating thought persisted in wrecking her morning. Meg grimaced and sat up in bed. *Maybe.* But she was human. Fallible. And this was one mistake she was willing to make. Because Derek was great in bed, but she wanted a male to be with her for more than just a quickie. *Okay. Usually more than a quickie.* She shrugged.

Ethan didn't know about her family. About her past. And that was nice. A kind, unassuming, attractive man who liked rainchecks. She could live with that. And maybe there would be more. It was a thought that made her smile.

Meg stood and smiled as her phone rang. Maybe that was the unassuming man now. She snatched the phone up.

"Hello," she said breathlessly.

"Hey, woman!" Erica's voice burst through the phone. "Have plans for the day?"

Meg ran her fingers through her fine hair and smiled. "No. I do not. What's on the books?"

"I'm meeting with a potential customer who wants to advertise on the site. I thought it would be best if we were both there. You up for it?"

"Sure." All the lustful thoughts of Ethan were pushed back a bit. Business was, after all, business. "What time's the meeting?" Meg glanced at the clock. Only a little after nine now.

"Eleven. We're having lunch at The Patio. He seems quite impressive. Claims to have found one of the secrets to a woman's sexual happiness."

Meg snorted. "Don't all men claim that?"

Erica laughed. "Yes, well. I suppose they do." Meg heard her rustling papers. "Colin something-or-other. Research mogul."

The name sounded familiar. Meg walked over to her closet. "Okay. I'll be there to lend a hand. If he's a lucrative client, we'll want to get him before someone else does."

"Precisely. See you this afternoon."

Meg hung up the phone and thumbed through her clothes. She finally pulled out a simply ivory cotton pantsuit. She rifled through her jewelry box until she found her mother's pearl necklace and earrings. Her hands moved over the pearls longingly. What she wouldn't give to have her mother back. Or her father. Hell, both of them.

The sadness crept over her with frigid fingers, and Meg tried to shake it off. Twice in two days the pain had hit her, and it wasn't going to do. Life dealt her a severe blow by taking both of her parents at once. And that had been compounded by the rumors which swirled around the deaths. People and reporters with small minds and big mouths.

Meg slammed her closet doors shut and told herself to let it go. The pain. The anger. *All of it. Now.* She rested her head against the door and breathed slowly in and out. When she was sure she wouldn't lose control, she stood slowly and went into the bathroom to take a shower. It wasn't a day for painful memories.

Time was of the essence. If this guy actually had a profitable business, then she and Erica could benefit from his advertising. If he only wanted his name on an adult site, Meg would firmly send him on his way.

She stepped into the shower and turned the water on hot. Steam built quickly, and Meg tried to let the heat melt away everything but the task at hand. This Colin fellow. She quickly lathered her hair and rinsed it. Then hurriedly washed her body. There were a few errands she needed to run before she arrived at The Patio.

Meg dialed her driver and told him to meet her at the house in thirty minutes. She winced and hung up the phone. She hated to use Carson, but half of business was about appearances. And Meg needed to be seen as a force to be reckoned with.

She quickly dressed and wound her hair in coils on her head. Meg grabbed her sunglasses and ivory clutch. She glanced once at the little black box by her bed and smiled. It would be different if this Colin fellow had more little black boxes. But she would reserve judgment until she heard what he had to say. One more check in the mirror, and she left the house.

* * * *

Carson smiled as he opened the door for her, and Meg slid inside. She thanked the driver who had been with her family for over twenty years and made herself comfortable.

"Where to, Miss Whittington?"

Meg chuckled. "I think you're about the only one who calls me that, Carson. It's nice to hear."

"Pleasure, Miss." He beamed at her through the rearview mirror.

"Take me to the Shaw Building first, please. I have a couple of forms I need to drop off. Then we'll swing by Classen Drive. There are papers that I need signed by the owner." Meg shuffled the belongings in her purse around. "Lunch at The Patio. I need to be there by eleven."

"Yes, Miss." Carson pulled out of the driveway and onto the road.

Meg fondly studied the back of his gray head before she turned back to the papers in her hand. She was going to buy the Shaw Building and set up the manager as the CEO. He was the only one in the upper echelon who had any idea of what needed to be done. The rest of them were busy lining their pockets and improving their golf games.

The golf course on Classen Drive would be sold to a new owner. Her father absolutely loved the course, but she had no use for it. The only stipulation in the new contract was that her father's name be left on the bunkhouse and golf carts. The new owner readily agreed.

Meg sighed and sat back. Part of her enjoyed this business part of her life. But part of her simply wanted to tutor students and be done. She was thankful for her business courses in college, though. She only used her lawyer on certain occasions. Not that Bart liked that, but he would live with it.

She tapped her fingers on her purse and watched the scenery roll by. *Busy day.* At least she could go back to normal on Monday. More students and perhaps a call from her new suitor, Ethan. Meg flushed and moved around in her seat. He had crossed her mind more than once while she was giving Derek a workout. The thought of those large hands moving over her body again. She shivered.

"You've arrived, Miss Whittington." Carson parked the car and walked around to her door. He opened it, and Meg stepped out. *Business now. Pleasure later.*

* * * *

Meg tucked back into the limo after the golf course buyer signed the papers. She opened her purse and touched up her makeup. Carson drove efficiently downtown, and Meg smiled. Maybe she would find something for her driver tomorrow while shopping. He was one of the most loyal people she had ever met.

"Carson."

"Yes, Miss?" His eyes instantly appeared in the rearview mirror.

"Is there something you've been longing for? A vacation, perhaps? A new book or three? Anything at all?"

Meg could see his blue eyes crinkle with a smile. "Trying to get rid of me, Miss?"

She chuckled. "Never. I only thought maybe you would like to get away for a few days."

"I'll let you know, Miss." He paused. "I might say the same for you."

"I'll take a vacation when school is out." Meg looked out the window. "Rather lonely when you have to go by yourself."

"Yes." Carson nodded and moved his eyes back to the road.

Meg smiled as he pulled right up to the curb outside The Patio. There were tables set out with large umbrellas over them. Waiters hovered expectantly over their guests. Drinks were refilled, and food served with barely a disturbance. She could see Erica with a dark-haired man at a table near the entrance. It was one of the best tables.

She couldn't see the man's face. She could, however, see that the suit was tailored and expensive. But that wasn't what caught her eye. Erica was laughing. Not the "polite" laughing. The one where a person laughed but didn't mean it. She was practically in tears from laughter.

Anybody that could charm her stern best friend couldn't be that bad. Carson opened her door, and Meg stepped out. People acted as if there were no limo curbside, but she could see glances from the corners of other's eyes.

Erica saw her then and waved briskly. The man beside her turned around, and Meg thought for a second that she was seeing things. Her mind flashed on the day she picked up Derek from winning the contest. *That man.*

This man. Was there. Dread spiraled up into her midsection, and Meg forced a smile to her lips. At least he wasn't kidding. He did have one of the keys to a woman's sexual happiness. *Oh shit.*

Meg walked briskly up to the table. The man stood, and Erica beamed up at her.

She extended her hand, and the man took it. "Colin Price."

"Margaret Whittington."

The man's jaw dropped, and Meg knew a moment of panic. He recovered quickly. "Are you the same Margaret Whittington that contributes to the American Research Society?"

"Yes." Meg relaxed a bit.

"That's marvelous!" Colin smiled. "You've helped make our project a viable option for women." He held Meg's chair out for her, and she sat down.

"You work for them?" Meg took a sip of water and was thankful for the cooling liquid. She needed to conclude this meeting as quickly as possible.

"Yes. We're but a small faction." Colin's smile broadened. "Small world, isn't it?"

"You don't know the half of it." Meg motioned to the waiter for a diet soda.

Erica pushed aside a portfolio to Meg. The leather-bound case burst with papers.

"Colin says that his facility has found an aide that will help women across the world with their sexual fantasies. It's fascinating."

"Colin?" Meg repeated and arched an eyebrow. She took the portfolio and smiled politely at the man.

"Mr. Price. Please tell me what you've told my associate. I'd love to hear it for myself."

He moved forward and smiled. "My pleasure." Colin motioned to the portfolio. "You see, my team and I have discovered a device that will not only be a woman's fantasy, it will enhance it."

Erica opened her mouth, but Meg held up her hand. "You've done research? Have a patent?"

Meg caught the hesitation even as Colin smiled. "We're in the process now. I simply wanted to line up a couple of sites, which would appreciate what we've done. I've done my research. Your site has the most hits of any its kind."

She caught the flattery but still pushed. "How do you even know that women will appreciate what you have to offer?"

His dark eyes gleamed. "We've done our research. Have test subjects. Collected data."

Meg kept the smile on her face at a cost. "What type of data, Mr. Price?"

"Audio. Visual. The whole nine yards."

Erica spoke up. "These women let you tape them? And listen to them?" Her voice was incredulous.

"There are standard consent forms."

Meg flashed back to all the papers she signed and tried not to wince. Maybe she'd be contacting her lawyer after all.

"We'll be looking over these papers and contacting you, Mr. Price."

His eyebrows shot up. "You don't want to discuss terms today?"

"I'm afraid not." Meg smiled.

The man's dark eyes narrowed. "I meant to ask. What exactly is your role in Erica's Erotic Findings?"

"That, Mr. Price, is really none of your business." Meg stood and tucked the portfolio under her arm. "But let's just say that I am interested in all types of businesses." She smiled down at Erica and bent to kiss her cheek.

"You two enjoy your lunch. I have appointments the rest of the afternoon." Her blue eyes met Erica's. "I'll call you later."

She strode away purposefully and thanked all that was good that Carson appeared almost instantly. She sank into the plush interior of the limo and opened the portfolio with shaking hands.

Reams of papers filled with numbers spilled across her lap. Meg picked up one and began reading. She didn't hear Carson open her door. She was too engrossed in the papers.

"Miss?"

Meg glanced up, startled. "I'm sorry." She tried to smile. Meg shuffled all the papers back into their case and stepped out of the limo. She hugged Carson and walked up to her front door.

A throbbing pain began in her right temple, and she knew it wouldn't be too long before she hated life. Not just Colin Price. *Conniving bastard.*

Just when she thought that people couldn't stoop any lower, some devious fuck of a researcher comes along and proves her wrong.

He'd tricked her that day. Used her attitude that she was in a hurry and the fact there were roughly two inches of paper before her to sign.

Meg shut the door behind her and walked upstairs to her medicine cabinet. She popped three ibuprofens and considered the facts.

She needed to have control of all of the research on her.

She needed to find out who was working with Colin and who had seen those tapes.

She needed to make sure none of this ever leaked out to the papers.

"Damn it." Meg sank onto her bed and closed her eyes. The portfolio lay in front of her, and she opened it again. What she didn't know could hurt her. She began reading.

* * * *

"Margaret Whittington is a bitch." Colin paced the room in front of Ethan and raked his hands through his dark hair. "I swear to God, if looks could kill, I'd be dead. And I don't understand it."

Ethan sighed. "So. You were charming the panties off of her associate, then what happened?"

"The cold-blooded bitch showed up and ruined everything. I would have gotten the contract if it weren't for her."

"You're being too harsh." Ethan calmly looked up at his friend and boss. "We haven't even decided what in the hell we're going to do with this information. We need the black box back so we can run some tests on it. Your meeting was premature anyway."

"Fuck that." Colin slammed his hand against the door.

Ethan watched Colin work off steam and hid his smile. Colin was hotheaded while Ethan was mellow and slow to anger. Another good combination.

"Listen." He held up his hands. "Let's let the test subject keep the box for the allotted time. We'll get it back. Run some diagnostics. Then we'll know if contracts and parties are the way to go. Okay?"

"We've worked too fucking hard to scrap this project." Colin nodded to himself. "That won't happen. Maybe tweaking some wires." He didn't even glance in Ethan's direction as he left the room mumbling.

Ethan rolled his eyes and brought up the data one more time. It still puzzled him that the toy seemed to be taking on characteristics that weren't programmed into it. He remembered the first moment when he realized he could make the toy actually feel like it was touching the subject. Colin damn near pissed on himself.

But this? The ability to actually be able to feel emotions? It wasn't a good thing. And partly, Ethan darkly admitted to himself, because the person the box felt something for was the same one he did.

He pulled up numbers and cross-referenced times and dates. Then he did a correlation with Meg's numbers and the toy's numbers. It did nothing to reassure him.

What would happen given another month or so? Would the toy actually communicate with Meg? Talk to her? Tell her what it thought?

Ethan hurriedly pulled up more data and immersed himself in trying to find the solution to a problem that could ruin his career and a budding romance.

Chapter 6

Meg lay on her stomach on her soft comforter and tried to sort the papers into manageable piles. Maybe she could handle this herself. The last thing she needed was a renewed interest in her life and past. Or a video of her having a very, very good time.

She growled low in her throat and shuffled the last of the papers into place. She pulled her ebony hair back into a ponytail and started with the large stack on her left.

There were spikes on reams of paper that showed blood pressure and heartbeats. Meg didn't know whether to laugh or cringe. Clearly written in one of the margins was *Test subject has above satisfactory results*. That was her, all right. The orgasmic overachiever.

She bit her lip and studied every inch of paper. There had to be a way to salvage this fucked-up mess. What would happen if she suddenly stopped using Derek? Meg pondered the possibilities. That would probably make the researchers suspicious. Exactly what she didn't need. The thought of someone watching her getting off gave her pause.

Part of her liked it very much. The part that had no sense of self-preservation.

At least that Colin asshole hadn't viewed the tapes. If he had, she was sure he would have stopped at nothing to make sure he got his way.

Meg needed to do a little research of her own. She swept the papers into a large briefcase and set it in her closet. Then she stripped down and crawled into bed under the covers. Meg slipped the earrings in her ears and turned the black box on.

Derek appeared instantly. He smiled down at her. "Meg."

"Derek." She patted the bed. He sank onto it and reached for her.

She held up her hands. "Just a second. How about a massage first?"

"Anything you wish." Derek's hands moved over her back with sure strokes, and Meg fairly purred. All her tension knots of the day loosened a bit.

"I have something to ask you," she murmured.

"Anything."

"Do you know who made you? Can you feel them?"

"Yes." The blue eyes stared intently at her. "I…feel things."

"Can you block them?"

Derek closed his eyes for a minute, and Meg held her breath.

"He is gone."

She blinked. "Are you sure? That quickly?"

"I've blocked the connecting wires. He can neither view nor hear us." Derek bent to kiss her bare back. "I like touching you, Meg."

She turned over and brought Derek's hands up to her breasts. His thumbs moved lazily over her nipples. Then he ducked his head to lick the nubs. His mouth trailed lazily down her body until it reached her belly button.

Meg held her breath as his tongue moved relentlessly against her sensitive flesh.

"And I like the way you taste."

She shivered at his words. And oh, how she loved to be tasted.

Derek's sure hands moved over her body, and Meg arched up into him. She threaded her hands through his hair and brought him closer.

Thoughts of Ethan flitted across her mind, and she bit back his name more than once. Derek was a wonderful toy, but she realized that getting involved with a little black box would be sheer stupidity.

He parted her legs and trailed his fingertips up from her knees to her thigh and higher. Softly he traced her folds and slipped two fingers inside her.

Meg cried out and thrust her hips up to meet his hand. She clenched the side of the bed with her hands as he worked those magic fingers inside her. And when he removed and licked them, she trembled at the rush of desire that flooded her body.

She opened her mouth to ask him to finish what he started when he shifted his body and slid the tip of his cock inside her pussy opening. Just an inch. Meg tried to shift and bring him farther inside her, but he wouldn't let her.

Another inch.

She trembled and grabbed his wrists on either side of her. "Please."

"You feel so right, Meg."

Derek bent and kissed the soft skin underneath her breast. Then he slid his cock fully into her.

Meg brought his mouth to hers and flicked her tongue against his soft lips. "You taste pretty good yourself."

She gazed into his blue eyes and smiled at his sure movements. "You don't have to worry about any missteps, do you?"

"I listen to your body, Meg." Derek stroked her hair softly behind her ear. "Isn't that what you want?"

She thought about Ethan for a second before Derek's next thrust took the thought clear out of her mind.

"Show me what I want, Derek."

"With pleasure."

* * * *

Meg wrapped a blue, silky robe around herself and slid her feet into a pair of lime green slippers. She pulled her hair back into a ponytail and padded downstairs. It was late, and the house was quiet.

Even though her body was relaxed, her head spun with all the possibilities of what she needed to do. How she needed to handle Colin Price, that snake in the grass. At least he didn't know who she was. Yet.

But if he found out, and she didn't have the upper hand, she would be screwed. And not in the good, "I've got a smile on my face" kind of way.

Meg pulled out a diet soda and popped the top on the can. She leaned back against her cabinet and let her mind wander. There were half a dozen ways to handle this debacle. She simply needed to decide on a plan of attack.

The phone rang and brought her out of her reverie.

"Hello?"

"Meg?"

She smiled. "Ethan?"

"Yeah. Listen. I'm sorry about the other night."

Meg tapped her fingers on the cabinet and smiled. "It's okay. I understand."

"I'd like to make it up to you."

Her smile broadened. That had definite possibilities. "And how would you like to do that?"

"I seem to recall a certain raincheck in effect."

Meg bit her lip to keep from laughing. "Uh huh."

"And I thought I could take you out to dinner." He paused. "And then possibly back to my place for a nightcap."

"A nightcap?" she repeated. "Would you like to be more specific?"

Ethan cleared his throat, and Meg covered the phone so he wouldn't hear her snort.

"I thought perhaps we could possibly finish what we started the other evening."

Ah. The man could get to the point.

"Sounds like a plan."

Meg heard a small sigh of relief and thanked God that men could still be a little unsure. It gave her hope.

136

"I'll pick you up around seven o'clock."

"I'll see you then, Ethan."

Meg hung up the phone and stood there in the kitchen. Ethan was into research. Maybe he could help her with her dilemma. Surely there were ethics that had to be adhered to for his line of work. She tapped her fingernails on the countertop again.

Then again, there might not be time for any discussions.

She smiled and walked back upstairs to bed.

* * * *

Meg woke up Sunday with plans for her day. She would spend at least a couple of hours straightening the house. She tended to let it slide a bit through the week. At one time, she had hired a maid service to come in once a week and tidy up. Then she caught the woman looking through papers that were none of her business. After a few ugly threats, Meg called her lawyer and threatened a lawsuit on the woman and the company.

Needless to say, Meg cleaned her own house from then on.

She pulled on a white ribbed tank and a pair of flannel Halloween boxers with pumpkins all over them. Meg pulled a blue headband through her hair and pulled out two socks from her drawer. One purple and one green. She slid them on and grinned. Nice to have a little color.

She took the stairs at a trot and hurried into the study. Meg opened the large, oak cabinet and admired her state-of-the-art stereo system. And with no neighbors close by, she could pretty much do whatever the hell she pleased decibel-wise.

Not much in the mood for country. Classical. Oldies. *Ahhh.* Meg found the CD she was looking for and popped it in.

Soon, the sounds of *The Eagles* filtered through her house. Meg bobbed her head along with the music and sang the words. Then she headed for the kitchen and a couple pieces of toast to help her make it through the day.

She snapped her fingers along with the music and ate her breakfast standing up. The study always came first on cleaning day. Then she'd work her way toward the front door. The patio if she had time.

Meg washed her toast down with diet soda and bopped back toward the point of cleaning origin. She polished the wood furniture and wiggled her hips with the beat. Took the duster and ran it along all her lovely toys in the closet. Vacuumed.

And even though it wasn't very warm in the house, she worked up a good sweat.

She wiped her forehead and went back into the kitchen for another drink. Meg made herself an ice water and checked the time. Not even eleven yet. Still plenty of time to finish her domestic duties before she worked on more pleasurable fare.

The knock on the door startled her, and she frowned. *Who in the hell would arrive on my doorstep on Sunday afternoon?*

Meg flung the door open and stood there in shock. It was Ethan. Looking comfortably handsome in black slacks and an emerald Henley. She picked her jaw up and smiled weakly.

"Um, hi. I thought our date was for later?" She licked her lips and cursed the Timing Fates. *Sadistic bastards.*

"It is. But I was in the neighborhood dropping something off." Ethan grinned broadly. "And then I realized I never asked you what you wanted for dinner. So I thought I would drop by. Am I interrupting something?"

"Just a small cleaning frenzy." Meg blew out a breath. "Listen. I'm not exactly dressed for company." She motioned to her clothes. "Hell, I'm not dressed to be seen. Period. So wherever you want to take me is fine. Really. I'll trust your judgment."

"Are you sure?" Ethan chuckled and ran his hands through his short red hair. "You could be taking your life into your own hands."

Meg shook her head. "Quit being charming. I'm standing here looking like a bag lady. The least you could do is leave me a little dignity."

She watched Ethan's eyes move over her body from her hair to her toes. They lingered on her full breasts, clearly outlined through her tank.

"Nothing at all wrong with your appearance." Ethan nodded. "Though I have to admit to wanting to ask if you're colorblind."

Meg laughed. "No, you ass. I like color."

"Very well. Then you're dressed accordingly." He paused. "A cleaning frenzy, you say?"

"Yes. Every Sunday, I bite the bullet and work on the house. Or try."

"Need any help?"

His blue eyes were earnest, and she found herself smiling. "I appreciate the offer, but you don't have to."

"I want to."

Meg heard the sincerity in his words and smiled. "You don't know what you're in for, Mr. Fields."

He bowed low. "At your disposal, Ms. White."

She grabbed his arm and brought him inside. "Don't say I didn't warn you."

"Mmm." He inhaled deeply. "Lemony fresh."

Meg laughed. "Like that, do you? Well, rest assured, there have been many lemons sacrificed this day." She turned and looked at him. "You're what? Six three or thereabouts?"

"Thereabouts."

"I need help in dusting some of the things in the study. I'm not quite tall enough." She looked at his nice shirt and slacks. "Um. You may want to rethink your offer."

"No." Ethan pulled the Henley off and had a plain white cotton shirt underneath it. "I'm fine."

Meg looked at his broad chest and suddenly forgot all about cleaning. Until Ethan looked at her expectantly.

"Where are the cleaning supplies?" He cocked his head to the side. "Ah. *The Eagles.* Good taste in music you have."

She grinned foolishly. "Thanks. Cleaning stuff is already in there. I'm going to start on the kitchen. Need anything to drink?"

"Tea, if you have it."

He followed her into the kitchen and waited. Meg poured his tea and handed it to him. She couldn't help but notice all the muscles and magnificent hands. *Later. Raincheck for later.* Right now she smelled of dust and dirt. Not exactly conducive to hot, monkey sex.

"Thanks." Ethan held his drink up and walked toward the study.

Meg sighed and looked around. The damn room wasn't going to clean itself.

* * * *

Half an hour later, she was on her hands and knees scrubbing when she heard Ethan walk into the doorway and stop.

Meg looked up, puzzled, until she saw what was in Ethan's hands. Or rather, what was overflowing in his hands.

Four of her favorite toys. Three vibrators in assorted colors and one butterfly stimulator.

"Shit," she muttered and stood quickly. *How could I have forgotten not to put all my toys up? Fuck.*

"I, uh—" Meg motioned to the toys and felt herself blushing. "Sorry about that."

Ethan's eyes were dark as they looked at her. "When you don't have rainchecks?"

She chuckled. "Something like that." Meg moved forward to take them when he held them up. She ran into his chest.

He dropped the toys on the kitchen table and looped an arm around her waist. "Care to show me?"

Heat flooded her body at the husky words. "I need a shower."

"Me, too."

Ethan's arm dropped, and he moved her back about a foot. His large hands started at her collarbone and moved toward her breasts. He cupped their heavy fullness in his palms and stroked her nipples.

"But I'm suddenly finding the cleaning second to what I really want to do."

"Oh, really?" Meg licked her lips. "And what would that be?"

"I want to give you a shower." Ethan's hands dropped and took hers in his. He tugged her toward the hallway and motioned up the stairs.

Meg nodded, and he kept her hand in his while they walked up the stairs. When they reached her room, they stepped inside.

Ethan's hands spanned her waist and gently lifted the tank over her head. Her breasts ached as stroked her. Then those hands pulled her shorts down, and she stepped out of them.

Next came her socks. Then her headband.

He never looked away from her as he undressed himself and led her into the bathroom.

Meg's pussy throbbed with anticipation. Ethan's cock stood at attention as he turned the shower on and checked the temperature. She grabbed the stiff length in her hand and stroked him up and down.

"You first." Ethan guided her inside the shower and put her back against the wall. Then he undid the showerhead and started at her feet. He lathered up a loofah and washed every inch of her skin. From her feet to her knees. And upwards. He stopped at her thighs and stood to wash her shoulders.

The water sluiced down her body, and Meg ached to have Ethan touch her with his mouth, his hands, or his cock. Preferably, all three.

The water massaged her skin, and she moaned as Ethan leaned in closer and rubbed his cock against her belly.

"You're beautiful," he murmured against her ear.

She shivered as he soaped her shoulders and moved to down her breasts. He circled each one and rubbed gently against the puckered nipples. Then he rinsed the soap off. Next, he slid the soap down to her belly and made small, slow circles.

It was exquisite torture.

Ethan put the loofah back and used the showerhead to rinse Meg off. Then he sank to his knees again. He handed the showerhead to Meg.

"Show me."

The softly worded invitation made her clit throb. Oh yes, she would show him. Then she would make sure he showed her. With every inch of his hard cock.

Meg looked down at him and spread her legs slowly. She parted her pussy with her left hand and gripped the showerhead with her right. She let the water massage her sensitive skin.

"Is that what you want?" Meg looked down at him and saw his eyes riveted to her wet pussy. "To watch me fuck myself with a showerhead?"

"Yes."

She nodded. "Good." Meg arched her hips to the spray and moaned. She felt her orgasm build, and her legs began to shake. The water hit her clit perfectly, and she couldn't wait for Ethan to watch her come.

She spread her legs further and hoped Ethan enjoyed the show.

Seconds later, Ethan took the showerhead from her hand and let it fall back against the tub.

Meg's breath heaved in her throat, but before she could utter a protest, Ethan replaced the water with his mouth.

She clutched his red hair in her hands as his tongue stroked her labia and slid upwards to circle her swollen clit.

He lifted her legs and put them over his shoulders as he gripped her ass and licked every inch of her pussy. She trembled and threw her head back at the sensations that raced through her body.

"Oh yes," she moaned. "Lick my pussy. Fuck me with your tongue." Meg pulled on her nipples with her left hand while guiding Ethan with her right. "I love the way that feels."

His tongue flicked against her clit with a relentless intensity that stole the breath from her body. She jerked up against his mouth with a scream and came over and over again. Her body shuddered uncontrollably against him.

Ethan slowly lifted his head and ran his tongue slowly up her pussy again. Aftershocks of pleasure rocked her body.

He gently slid her legs down and wrapped them around his waist.

Meg looked up at him and brought his mouth down to hers. She kissed him lazily as he slid his cock in to the hilt and stayed there.

"I want to fuck you, Meg. Feel your pussy tighten around my cock. Hear you scream my name," he murmured against her mouth. He slid his cock out and thrust back in. Over and over again.

His large cock stretched her to the limit with every thrust, and she shuddered as his fingers dug into her ass.

"Tell me what you want." Ethan bent and sucked her nipple into his hot mouth. Then he moved his hand down between their bodies and continued thrusting. His finger traced over her spread legs and stroked her.

Meg looked down between their bodies and watched his cock slide in and out of her. She arched to meet every thrust.

"You like to watch my cock in your pussy?" Ethan lifted her hips and slammed his hard cock into her faster.

Her eyes met his. "Yes."

His hands gripped harder as he stroked smoothly inside her. The tension built inside her again with a promise of more pleasure, and Meg held onto every second of it.

She came with a jerk and reveled in the feel of Ethan's hard cock inside her. He followed her with a shout, and she watched his face clench in pleasure.

Ethan gently lay her down and picked up the showerhead again. He washed them both off and bundled her tightly in a towel.

"You look good wet."

Meg laughed and kissed his cheek. "Thanks."

Ethan wound a towel around his waist and guided her back into her bedroom. Meg sat on the edge of her bed, and he sat beside her.

"It wasn't my intent to come over and have my way with you."

She smiled. "Well. Damn it all."

Ethan glanced at her and chuckled. "Okay. Maybe deep down."

"Regrets?"

"None." He lay back on the bed and studied her. "Well. One."

Meg arched an eyebrow.

"It didn't happen sooner."

She rolled over on her side and grinned. "I like a straightforward man. It simplifies matters."

Ethan stroked her wet hair gently. "Mind if I ask a question?"

She cocked her head to the side. "Depends on the question."

"Why all the hardware?"

"Ah." Her blue eyes sparkled with laughter. "You're wondering why a woman needs so many toys. What a male question."

"Ouch." Ethan winced. "Parts of me have been wounded."

Meg shrugged out of her towel and walked leisurely to her closet. She pulled on a blue silk robe and belted it. When she turned, she grinned. Ethan's eyes were riveted to her.

"Come here, Ethan." She held out her hand, and he stood. He slid his hand into hers and followed her downstairs.

No one had ever glimpsed her naughty treasure chest. *Um, cavern.* But she was dying to show Ethan and gauge his reaction.

Meg stopped in front of the hidden closet and turned to Ethan. "What you're about to see has been gazed upon by no one. We can have a question/answer session after you come out of your state of shock."

He opened his mouth, and she gently placed her fingers over his lips. Meg opened the door and stepped back.

Ethan breathed in sharply, and she tried extremely hard not to snicker.

"Can I touch them?"

She nodded.

There were five shelves crammed full of boxes of every sexual toy known to man and retailers. Vibrators, dildos, stimulators, dolls, and lubes.

Ethan would pick up one, look at it, and put it back. He worked slowly. Methodically. Shelf to shelf.

Meg left him to his own devices and walked into the kitchen to pour herself a diet soda. She sat at the kitchen table and waited.

Ethan walked slowly into the kitchen about twenty minutes later. He grabbed a soda out of the refrigerator and sat across from her. His blue eyes were unfathomable.

"I'm either extremely turned on or scared shitless."

Laughter poured out of Meg before she could stop herself. Tears leaked from her eyes and slid down her cheeks. She stood and tore off a paper towel to dab her eyes. When she turned to study him, he nodded.

"I'm serious."

"I know." Meg threw the paper towel away and sat again. "I do research, Ethan. The same as you."

Panic fluttered in his chest for a minute.

"I help a friend decide which toys are best and so forth." She grinned. "And it helps between rainchecks."

"A lesser man would probably be a tad bit intimidated."

"Believe me." Meg covered his hand with hers. Her blue eyes were sincere. "You have nothing to be worried about." Memories of their pleasure play filtered through her mind.

"I know."

At the bland statement, Meg's mouth dropped open. She threw back her head and laughed. "Oh my God!" She wiped her eyes again. "Too funny."

Ethan glanced back toward the study and then at the kitchen clock. "It's early yet. And I saw a couple of items that I would sorely like to try out."

Meg arched an eyebrow. "Oh, really?"

"Come here, woman." Ethan crooked his finger. "You and I have business."

* * * *

Meg watched Ethan sleep and smiled. His red hair was slightly tousled, and she itched to run her fingers through it. After all, they had made love for hours. She glanced at the edge of the little black box underneath her scarf. She needed to explain to Colin Price, egomaniac, that it wasn't all about the orgasm.

Though, Meg admitted to herself, that was certainly a perk.

She stood and walked quietly to the door. She glanced back and stopped. Ethan's large frame in her bed was a nice sight. A sight that she might want to try out on more than just a one-night basis.

Meg walked downstairs in a matching tank set with elves all over it.

They never made it to a restaurant, but instead, ate sandwiches in her kitchen before heading back upstairs.

It was almost five in the morning now. She had students arriving from ten o'clock on. And Ethan would have to go back to his house to change clothes before work.

Meg tapped her fingernails on the table and stared into space. The whole "black box debacle", as she now thought of it, was foremost in her mind. She wanted to get Ethan's opinion on the whole thing, but she thought one major shock for the evening was more than enough.

And her toy closet definitely qualified.

She walked over and started her coffeemaker. More than likely, Ethan would need some caffeine before he headed back to his own house. Then she opened the refrigerator and took some eggs out. Bacon next. Some bread. Good thing she actually went to the grocery store the other day.

Half an hour later, Ethan tumbled through the kitchen door, yawning.

"I hate mornings," he muttered.

Meg put a cup of coffee in front of him and smiled. "I'm not particularly fond of them myself." She placed a full plate in front of him, and he looked up at her with gratitude.

"You are without equal."

"I know." Meg chuckled and put the dirty dishes in the sink. She could hear Ethan eat and make little groans of pleasure between bites. She finished the dishes and turned to see him take his last bite.

"I've got to go." Ethan's voice held regret. He stood and stretched.

Meg's eyes traced over his broad chest, and she bit back a sigh of regret herself.

"I'll try and call later, depending on my schedule." He walked over and brushed his lips softly over hers.

"Have a good day." Meg wound her arms around his neck and rested her head against his heart. She slid her arm down around his waist, and they walked to the front door.

Ethan walked outside and waved.

Meg waved back and shut the front door. At least her Monday started on a high note.

* * * *

It went rapidly downhill.

Shannon was uncommonly moody and fought Meg every inch of the way on studying. Finally, Meg threw up her hands.

"You win! I give. Now tell me what's wrong."

Shannon's green eyes grew moist. "I hate my life."

"Honey." Meg moved around to the side of the table Shannon sat at and drew her close. "What's so bad that you feel like that?"

"Danny's dating Carey!"

Shannon buried her head against Meg's chest and sobbed. Meg stroked her hair and sighed. *First love sucked. Second love wasn't so hot, either. And teenage hearts were so fragile.*

"I'm so sorry, hon."

Shannon lifted her head. "And that's not the worst part!" She sniffled. "Carey only liked him after I said I did." She covered her face with her hands and sobbed more.

Meg's mouth flattened into a thin line. Cruelty had many forms. And betrayal ranked in the top five.

She patted Shannon's back and tried to think of the right words. Unfortunately, none of them would ease the pain.

"Want to talk about it?"

Shannon sighed and wiped at her tears. "He's only dating her because she'll put out."

"Shannon!" Meg's mouth dropped open. "What did you just say?"

"It's true." Her green eyes were defiant. "I overheard two guys talking about it in the hall."

"Oh Lord." Meg rubbed her temples. "First, do no repeat that."

"Even if it's true?"

"At all." Meg's voice was stern. "I know that you're hurting, but hurting someone else will not make you feel better. And it makes you no better than her." Her blue eyes softened. "Do you understand what I'm saying?"

"I think so."

"Second." Meg shook her head. "We have no control over someone else's actions. We can only work within our lives. And third, there is this little thing called Karma."

"Karma?" Shannon's eyes were puzzled.

"What goes around comes around, sugar. Every time."

"How long does that take?"

Meg sighed. "No specific time frame. But believe me. It'll happen."

* * * *

Meg finished with her students around four in the afternoon and sported a raging headache. It was simply one of those days. She changed out of her slacks and conservative blouse for another tank set. This one had fairies flying about.

She took her headache pills and sat at the kitchen table, nursing a diet soda, which she was quite sure wasn't helping her headache.

The phone rang, and she winced.

Meg fumbled for it.

"Hello?"

"Meg. Hi!" Erica's perky voice filtered through the phone. "So. Tell me what's going on. Why are you so reticent about Colin's advertising on our site?"

Meg was in no mood to mince words. "Gee, Erica. Probably because he has tapes of me fucking the hell out of a projection."

Chapter 7

Complete silence from the other end of the phone.

And then, in an incredibly hushed voice, "What did you just say?"

"Are you doing anything right now?"

"No."

"Then come over. Front door is unlocked. I'll explain everything when you get here." Meg hung up the phone and calculated on any other day, it would take Erica fifteen minutes to arrive at her house. She was betting the new record would probably be five. She wasn't disappointed.

Erica blew through the front door approximately six minutes later. She strode into the kitchen and sat down quickly.

"Tell all." Her blue eyes were wide, and her auburn hair tousled.

"I entered a contest. A contest for the Ultimate Sex Toy."

Erica nodded. "Okay."

"Anything but okay." Meg blew out a breath. "I won."

Her friend frowned but didn't say a word.

"I won a projection that I can actually feel. I put earrings in my ear, and I can feel him touch me."

Erica blinked twice. "I'm not sure I understand."

Meg made a decision right then. "Follow me upstairs. And I promise you an experience you will never forget."

She stood, and Erica followed. They walked slowly upstairs and into Meg's bedroom. She plucked the earrings from the nightstand and held them up.

"Put these in your ears."

Erica opened her mouth, but Meg shook her head. "Just do it."

She put both earrings in and waited. "Okay. Seriously. They're nice earrings. But what the hell do they have to do with anything?"

"Just wait." Meg walked over and switched the black box on.

Erica shrieked and held her heart to her chest. She looked at Meg. "Oh my God! I can see a man."

"Not only can you see him. You can feel him." Meg touched Erica's arm. "Ask him to turn the visual off."

"Visual off."

"He says it is. And he asked where you are."

"Tell Derek I'm right here. But that I want him to help you today."

Erica repeated the words and then gasped.

Meg smiled as she watched the one-sided scene. Erica's eyes were closed, but pleasure was written all over her face. She sank to the bed and sighed.

"Is he nude?"

Erica nodded and looked at Meg. "He's beautiful."

"I know." She started to unbutton Erica's blouse. "Your turn."

Erica's eyes darkened. "And what do you think you're doing?"

"Helping." Meg winked and finished undoing Erica's blue blouse. She parted it and touched the white frilly bra underneath. "I want you to verbally tell Derek what you want."

Erica's hands moved up, and Meg watched, fascinated. Her friend seemed to be holding someone, though Meg couldn't actually see him.

"Kiss me, Derek."

Meg ran her hands down Erica's breast and cupped them in her hand. She bent down and sucked one through the silky fabric, and Erica arched up.

She opened her eyes, hazy with desire. "He knows what you're doing. Where you're touching me."

"Good." Meg flicked her tongue across Erica's nipple. "I want to watch him fuck you."

Erica trembled at the words. She reached up and pulled Meg's hair out of the ponytail and brought her mouth down.

"Only if I get to watch him fuck you."

Meg licked Erica's lips with a grin. "Sounds like a deal."

She reached around and undid Erica's bra. Now her friend only wore blue slacks and sandals. Meg took the sandals off and moved back up.

She stroked Erica's hard nipples. "Tell Derek what you want. Where you want his mouth. His hands. His cock."

"Lick my nipples." Erica threw her head back and moaned.

Meg licked her lips and watched her friend being pleasured. She slowly unsnapped Erica's pants and pulled them down her legs. The small blue thong Erica wore barely covered her. And Meg pulled it aside to look at her friend's aroused pussy.

The dark hair was trimmed neatly, and Meg felt her clit throb. She moved a hand up Erica's thigh and between her legs. She stroked the silky lips and slid one finger up to circle Erica's clit.

"Oh." Erica spread her legs farther and arched her back.

"Tell him to eat your pussy, Erica."

Meg heard Erica say the words, and she moved slightly out of the way. She watched as Erica spread her legs further. Her hand moved up, as if to grab someone, and she cried out.

"That's so nice." Meg put her hand on Erica's left knee and spread her legs more. "Tell me what he's doing"

"He's sliding his tongue in my pussy." Erica trembled. She shut her eyes. "Licking my clit."

"Yes." Meg flicked her tongue against Erica's hard nipple and sucked it deeply into her mouth. "I like the way you spread your legs for him. Letting him fuck you with his mouth." She licked Erica's nipples and watched as Erica lifted her hips in the air over and over again.

"I want to hear him make you come."

"He…" Erica's hips snapped up, and she cried out as her orgasm ripped through her.

"Mmmm." Meg slid her hand down and rubbed Erica's pussy. "You're not done yet."

Erica's eyes opened hazily. "I don't know how much more I can take."

Meg spread Erica's legs. "Tell him to fuck you, Erica. With his big cock. Tell him to pound the hell out of your pussy."

Erica shuddered with pleasure. "Fuck me, Derek. With your cock." She bent her knees and whimpered, "Oh, yes."

Meg took her tank top off and rubbed her hand over her aching breasts. She was wet with wanting Derek to fuck her.

She pushed her nipple into Erica's mouth. "Suck it."

Erica latched on quickly and flicked her tongue against the hard pebble. She reached up and kneaded the other one.

Meg leisurely moved and slid her mouth down Erica's body. "Does his cock feel good?"

"Yes." Erica shuddered.

She stopped mere inches from Erica's pussy and licked her friend's soft skin. Meg slid her finger down to Erica's clit and made small circles. "Come all over his cock."

Erica cried out and shook with the force of her orgasm. She trembled for at least another minute on the bed and then became still.

"I think I lost consciousness."

Meg chuckled. "It's a possibility." She glanced up at her friend's face.

Erica slowly opened her eyes. "My turn." She took out the earrings and handed them to her friend. Her nails traced over Meg's hard nipples.

"You're beautiful."

"So are you." Meg smiled. "Too bad we didn't experiment in college."

Erica threw back her head and laughed throatily. "You're too good a friend to be my girlfriend."

"Exactly."

Meg slid the earrings in and sighed with pleasure at the sight of Derek. He moved quickly to her.

"Did I satisfy your friend?"

"Yes."

Derek's hands moved between her legs and touched her swollen clit. "You're on the edge of an orgasm. Your body is tight. I can feel it."

"Then make me come."

Derek turned her around and bent her over the bed. "Is your friend still here?"

Meg looked at Erica who still lay on the bed. "Yes."

"Then let her watch."

Derek sank to his knees and moved his mouth against her willing pussy. His hands gripped her hips as he fucked her with his tongue.

Erica moved closer and slid her hands across Meg's breasts. "Tell me what he's doing."

"Licking my pussy. Deeper and deeper." Meg worked her clit against his mouth for barely a minute before she came with a cry and shuddered. She barely caught her breath when he stood and slid his cock where his mouth just was.

"Yes. Fuck me, Derek."

Erica shifted to the side of Meg and slid her finger between Meg's legs. "I want to feel you come against my hand." She rubbed back and forth across the swollen bud.

Derek's balls slapped against her ass as he rammed his cock into her over and over again.

Meg felt her orgasm build until she thought she would die from the pleasure. And when her body shook again, she screamed at the force of it.

She collapsed on the bed and rolled over slowly.

Derek looked down at her with a smug look on his face.

"I didn't know projections could be so self-satisfied."

"I am different."

Erica propped herself up on her elbows and looked at Meg. "I just figured out what I want for Christmas." Her blue eyes shone.

Meg waved at Erica with her hands. "You're a degenerate." She looked back at Derek. "What exactly do you feel?"

"Changed." Derek stood nude before her. "I want things."

"What's he saying?" Erica looked off into space.

"Shhh." Meg looked at Derek. "Go on."

He sat beside her on the bed. "I like you, Meg." His hand tangled through her long hair. "A lot."

Meg's eyes widened. *What exactly had those researchers done? Infused a thinking, feeling being into a simple gadget?*

"Was that part of your programming?"

"I do not know."

Meg bit her lip and glanced at Erica. "I need to go downstairs, Derek. I'm going to take my earrings off."

He nodded. "I will see you later."

She took off her earrings and looked at Erica. "We've got more problems."

* * * *

Meg paced her kitchen floor while Erica sat at the table and ate a sandwich.

"How can you just sit there and eat?" Meg threw up her hands and glared.

"Same way you can pace the floor." Erica finished the last bite and pushed the plate away from her. "So that's what you've been doing here."

"Not exactly."

Erica's eyes grew large and then narrowed. "What do you mean? Not exactly?"

"I won Derek and immediately started using him." Meg bit the inside of her cheek. "Then I've found someone who I am truly starting to care for. A real man."

Erica shook her head back and forth. "I can't keep up with you."

"I like Derek. And God knows he's a great fuck. But he's a machine. Not a person. And Ethan..." Meg trailed off.

"Ethan what?" Erica frowned. "And Ethan who?"

"I picked him up in a grocery store." Meg smiled. "He's a rather inept shopper."

"You picked up a man in a grocery store?" Erica's mouth dropped open. "Holy shit, Meg. Have you lost your mind?"

"I was lonely!" She shook her head. "Having an orgasm is great. But I like the afterwards, too. Cuddling. Touching his skin. The after perks."

"And you've had these after perks with Ethan?"

"Once."

"And does he know you're fucking the shit out of a kinky projection?"

Meg sighed. "No. But he does know about my toy closet."

"Wow." Erica blinked. "That's a first."

"Tell me about it."

Erica cocked her head to the side. "And does he know who you really are?"

"Who?" Meg's voice was bitter. "Margaret Elizabeth Whittington? The girl whose father killer her mother for money? No. He isn't aware of that, yet."

Erica stood and hugged Meg tightly. "You know that isn't how it happened."

"I'm just so damn bogged down with everything. This whole Derek debacle. And the fucking tapes!" Meg growled. "That Colin guy has tapes of me and Derek. How do you think that will play out?"

"Like shit." Erica sighed.

"Yeah." Meg's mouth flattened in disgust. "I need to get on top of this situation as quickly as possible. I believe

I owe Colin Price a visit soon. He and I need to come to an understanding and quickly."

* * * *

Ethan typed in the master code to his files and tapped his fingers impatiently on the metal desk. This whole situation was a clusterfuck of the highest order. And he had no idea, right this second, how to fix it.

All the research put into making a woman's Ultimate Sex Toy was backfiring at a rapid rate of speed. And Colin was in hyper asshole mode.

He haunted Ethan's door every second he was there. Asked him annoying questions. And generally became the biggest pain in the ass Ethan ever had the misfortunate to be around.

The homepage loaded, and Ethan quickly accessed the UST files.

Pages of data began scrolling past. Ethan quickly found pieces of what he was looking for and copied the files on another disk. He would take them home and pick through them with a fine-tooth comb. There was no way in hell he would let this research simply disappear.

"Well. I'm glad to see you've finally graced me with your presence."

Ethan spun in his chair and looked at his friend in the doorway. "You look like shit." And he did. His normally elegant appearance had taken a turn for the worse. Colin's white shirt had a stain on it and was wrinkled beyond repair. His normally perfect hair stuck out from his head in several odd angles, and his eyes were bloodshot.

"Fuck you." Colin staggered in and collapsed in the chair next to Ethan. "If we don't find and fix this, we can say goodbye to all our funding. I have forty-eight hours to present my findings to the board." He sighed. "We're screwed."

Ethan wrinkled his nose. "First. Find a breath mint. Second. I'll find the glitch. I'm copying files and taking them home with me."

Colin slammed his hand on the desk. "Maybe this test subject screwed around with the toy's wiring. Took him apart. Studied him. Could be a fucking scam."

"Meg wouldn't do that."

Colin's eyebrows winged up. "What did you just say?"

Ethan's stomach lurched. "I'm quite sure the test subject wouldn't do anything like that." He motioned to the numbers in front of him. "When would she find the time?"

"That mousy brunette nympho could be playing us." He studied Ethan. "And how did you know her name?"

"She told the projection."

Colin still studied him suspiciously. "I'd like to view the tapes."

"No."

Colin blinked. "I don't believe I heard you right."

"You did." Ethan ran his hands through his short, red hair. "Listen. I've got it. No need for you to look at the tapes. You need some sleep. Let me work on this for a while."

"No. First we're going to discuss the fact that you're denying me access to research. Then we're going to go over the interesting tidbit that you called the test subject by her first name. What the fuck is going on?"

"I've met her." Ethan avoided Colin's eyes.

"Son of a bitch!" Colin stood up and growled. "This is unreal."

"It was an accident. At the grocery store." Ethan stood, too. "It's a machine malfunction. Nothing more. Nothing less. I'll fix it."

Colin glared at Ethan. "Did you fuck her?"

Ethan stood stock-still. "What I did or didn't do with Meg is none of your fucking business. And since you're my best friend, I won't knock your teeth down your throat." He pushed the disc out and slid it in his jacket. "I'll call when I have news."

* * * *

Meg tutored the next day until four o'clock. Then she changed into a silky, baby blue pantsuit and heels. She left her hair down and hurried out to her car. The events of the previous evening weighed heavily on her mind.

She still hadn't turned off the box. *Was that good? Or bad? Was Derek actually bored?* Meg rubbed her temple and cursed Colin Price once more for good measure. *Arrogant, sneaky bastard.*

She pulled out of her driveway and drove toward Ethan's house. She missed him. And maybe he would know something about her situation to help. She'd be suitably vague. Skirt around the real issue. But maybe Ethan could give her an insight she didn't have right now.

Meg pulled into his driveway fifteen minutes later and checked herself in the mirror. She looked at her watch and cursed. She should have called. This whole sex toy mess scrambled her brain.

She stepped out of her car and walked quickly up to the front door. Meg knocked twice and waited.

Ethan yanked the door open with a scowl. "What?"

Meg blinked. "I'm sorry. I should have called."

His jaw dropped open. "What are you doing here?"

"I'm sorry." Meg took a step backwards and held her hand up. "I should have called. My impetuous nature."

She turned on her heel and strode quickly back to her vehicle.

"Meg. Wait!" Ethan trotted after her and blocked her path. "I'm sorry. You took me by surprise."

"I didn't mean to interrupt." She tried to smile.

"Come inside." Ethan put his arm around her and guided her back up the path. "You're fine." He moved her closer and kissed her head. "I'm always glad to see you."

Meg stepped inside and hung her purse and jacket on the coat rack. "I'll only stay a minute." She looked at Ethan's disheveled appearance. "I think my timing is rather poor today."

Ethan grimaced. "Just because I look like death warmed over doesn't mean much." He waved his hand around. "Work. Lots of it. Troubleshooting a small problem."

"Ah." Meg tapped her fingernails on the wall. "I have a couple of questions to ask you about your work. If you don't mind."

Ethan swallowed convulsively. "Uh. Sure. Just let me clean up a bit. I'll be right back." He scurried down the hall and slammed his bedroom door.

Ethan reappeared fifteen minutes later wearing blue jean shorts and a dark green T-shirt. His red hair was still wet. He walked over and stood by the couch. "Can I get you something to drink?"

"A diet soda, please."

Meg watched him go with a smile. She inhaled deeply. He smelled good enough to taste. She clenched her fist in her hand and told herself not to jump the nice researcher until after she had some possible answers. Otherwise, she was likely to forget.

Ethan came back and handed Meg her drink. He popped the top on his beer and sat beside her. "What's wrong?"

She took a deep breath. "I have a friend who has some questions about research." Meg prayed the words didn't sound as stupid as she thought they did. "Think you can help?"

Ethan's stomach dropped, and he fought to keep the interested look on his face. This situation could become very bad very quickly.

"Anything in particular?" he asked casually.

"Well." Meg fiddled with her soda and tried to find the right words. "Aren't there ethical issues? She's afraid she'll be suckered into making bad decisions based on false information." Her blue eyes met Ethan's.

He steadied his voice. "Usually there are forms that have to be filled out by test subjects. She will be required to sign consent forms and the like." Ethan shifted on the couch.

"But what if she's already signed the papers and finds out the data will be embarrassing and improper?" Meg blinked back sudden tears.

Ethan stood quickly and moved away from the couch. He turned back a couple of minutes later. "It sounds like quite a mess. Perhaps she should simply quit the study. That might be best."

"Perhaps." Meg frowned and pushed her ebony hair back behind her ear. She motioned to the cushion beside her. She pushed the study from her mind. Right now, she needed Ethan. "And maybe you can come over here and keep me company."

He walked back over and sat down.

Meg leaned forward and brushed her lips against his. "Where have you been, Ethan?"

"Work," he mumbled. His large, strong hands moved up to bring her mouth closer, deeper. His tongue stroked hers while his hand moved down to cup her breast through the silky blue of her shirt.

"So soft," he whispered.

Meg's head fell back as Ethan moved from her mouth to her throat. His lips skimmed along her pulse as his left hand slowly unbuttoned her shirt. He nipped the delicate flesh while his hand cupped her breast and stroked the hardened nipple.

She arched her back and clutched Ethan's hair with her left hand while her right covered his on her breast.

His hot breath on her neck made her moan in excitement. And then his hand slipped lower to stroke her pussy through her thin silk pants.

Meg spread her legs and rubbed herself against his hand as he moved his mouth down to close on her exposed nipple. He sucked and licked the hard nub while she writhed and moaned beneath him.

"Ethan."

He lifted his head and Meg moved forward to undo his shirt and shrug it off his shoulders. Her hands splayed over his hard chest, and she licked her lips.

"Such a beautiful man."

Ethan chuckled low. "You're the beautiful one."

Meg moved forward and licked his nipple while her hand moved lower to stroke his cock through his pants. She pushed Ethan back a bit and slowly unzipped his pants. She pulled her shirt over her head and threw it on the ground.

"I want to taste you, Ethan."

The soft words made him groan and shift on the couch.

Meg pulled his jeans down and slid them off his legs. Then she moved forward and rubbed her breasts against his hard cock.

Ethan thrust his hips up, and she smiled.

She pulled his underwear down slowly and licked her lips as his cock was freed and sprang to attention. Meg grasped it in her hand and looked up at Ethan. Then she lowered her head and licked the tip.

Ethan clutched the back of her head as she licked and sucked his shaft while her hands cupped his balls. While she worked her tongue against every inch of him, she gripped his hips.

Meg flicked her tongue against the underside of his cock head, and Ethan groaned in pleasure.

"Enough." Ethan lifted her head, and she smiled. Her tongue came out and licked the side of her lips. He groaned.

"You're not the only one who wants a taste." Ethan moved forward and pushed Meg gently back on the cushions. He pulled her bra down completely but left it hooked. The fabric pushed her breasts up, and he smiled.

Then he lowered his mouth to flick his tongue against the sensitive nubs. Meg clutched his shoulder and gasped with pleasure. He sucked on each in turn and slid his hands down to take her silky blue pants off.

Meg lifted her ass while he made quick work of her pants. Ethan hooked his fingers in her underwear and took them off with one quick stroke. She lay bare to his eyes.

Ethan moved down to her ankles and winked. Then he moved his mouth slowly up her legs. He stopped to flick the underside of her knees, and she moaned. Her pussy throbbed with anticipation as his mouth moved nearer.

He gently parted her legs and hooked his arms under her knees and exposed her pussy to his gaze. Then he lowered his mouth and flicked his tongue against her swollen clit.

Meg cried out as his tongue moved against her in a sure rhythm that had her spreading her legs further. She clutched the back of his head and worked her pussy against his hot mouth.

He sucked her deeper and deeper into his mouth, and Meg came with a cry and shudder that left her limp and breathless. When her body stopped trembling, she looked lazily at Ethan.

"I hope you don't think you're done."

Ethan kissed her inner thigh and shook his head. "Not a chance." He grabbed her hips and flipped her body over in an instant.

Meg laughed and looked up over her shoulder at him. "Well, aren't you gifted?"

"You don't know the half of it." Ethan winked at her and gripped her hips. Then he shifted the tip of his cock to her pussy and pushed gently.

Meg moved her ass back, and he slid his hard cock as deeply as he could into her. She dug her fingers into the cushion below her and whimpered.

Ethan's fingertips dug into her hips as he moved slowly out and then back inside her. He leaned over and kissed her back as he stroked his hard cock in and out of her. Then he moved farther down and cupped her breasts in his hand while he fucked her from behind.

She slid her hand down between her legs and stroked her clit while Ethan's cock pleasured her.

His stroked increased, and she started to shake as her orgasm built quickly.

"Come for me, Meg. Come all over me."

Meg's fingers moved faster as Ethan told her what he wanted her to do. She came with an orgasm that slammed her ass against Ethan. He pumped his cock twice more into her before he came, too.

They collapsed like a stack of cards, and she swiveled so that her breasts flattened against Ethan's hard chest.

She stroked his damp hair and smiled. "You make me forget my worries."

Ethan lifted his head and smiled. "You make me forget the world."

She chuckled. "Thanks. I think." Meg stretched luxuriously. "I'm rather glad I interrupted you now."

"Me, too." Ethan kissed one breast then the other. "I like you naked on my couch. There are so many possibilities."

Meg grinned down at him. "I like you, Ethan."

His blue eyes flashed. "I like you, too, Meg."

She glanced up at the clock on the wall and winced. "Okay. Not to just pick your brains and then fuck them out, but I've got to go. I have a lot of things to do this evening."

"Normally, I'd invade your space." Ethan grimaced. "But I have my own problems to attend to this evening."

Meg sat up. "You will be over tomorrow, won't you? It's Brad's session."

"Wouldn't miss it."

She nodded, pleased. "Good. I think he really likes you. And his work has improved since that first session."

"He's a good kid." Ethan watched her stand and assemble her clothing again.

Meg winked. "Open invite to disrobe me. Just in case you need a raincheck."

Ethan smiled. "I'll definitely keep that in mind."

She pulled on her clothes and ran her fingers through her tousled hair. She watched Ethan pull on his pants and shirt. After he was dressed, he walked her to the front door.

"Don't let your friend worry about the research thing." Ethan smiled. "I'm sure it will work out."

"Thanks." Meg leaned forward and kissed him softly. She walked down the path and turned to wave. He waved back and waited until she pulled out of the driveway to shut the door.

* * * *

Ethan shut the door and then kicked it for good measure. His toe throbbed painfully from the effort. "Fuck."

Sure, Meg. Don't worry a bit about the million dollars of research riding on this experiment. Or the fact I'm starting to fall in love with you. Or any of that.

Ethan shut his eyes for a minute and tried to focus his thoughts. How could he fall in love with a test subject? But she wasn't just a test subject. She was the woman who made him feel as if he were ten foot tall and bulletproof.

The woman who looked to him for answers and touched parts of him that no other had.

"Why must my life suck?" Ethan words echoed in the room. But there was no ready answer.

* * * *

Meg drove home with a satisfied smile on her face. Derek was a great toy, but Ethan gave her more than sex. He gave her parts of himself. Her smile faded. It sounded exactly like what Derek wanted to share.

"Son of a bitch." Meg pulled into her driveway and sat in her car for a minute or two. She had to collect her thoughts. Fix this fucked-up mess. She stepped out of her car and strode into the house.

First things first. She needed a list of items that would make this situation a bit easier. Meg walked into the study and sat at her desk. She calmly removed a notebook from the top drawer and took her favorite pen out of the coffee mug on the desk.

She needed to contact Colin Price. She would, of course, have to reveal that she repeatedly screwed the pants off an experiment. But at least she was in the position to remind him that a lot of her money went into the project. Then she would have the supreme pleasure of reaming him over the fact that he tricked her. And besides,

Meg jotted down notes, apparently his experiment was beginning to have a mind of his own.

Meg's blue eyes shot upward. Maybe she should turn the box off. At least until she had some semblance of an idea of what to do. She bit her lip and sorted through her thoughts. Derek was probably bored. Meg pushed her chair back and strode quickly upstairs. She stopped in her doorway and looked around. Derek was there, somewhere. A small feeling of guilt crept through her. Meg hurried over and switched the box off. Her shoulders slumped in relief after she did it. Maybe he was resting now.

She rolled her eyes and sat on her bed. The Ultimate Sex Toy was a great concept. *But what did you do when the toy started to have a mind of its own?*

Meg sighed and stood up. There was a list downstairs with her name written all over it. Now all she had to do was fill it in.

* * * *

Ethan drove to Meg's house the next day and parked in the driveway. He glanced at the house and grimaced. He worked on the experiment until the wee hours of the morning and still no progress. It was as if his world were shrinking. And he had to keep everything balanced before they started bumping up against one another.

Two hours sleep wasn't cutting it. When he drove back home, he planned on falling into bed and not getting up until the next day. Then he would take his problems back to the lab and dissect them there.

He stepped from his car and ran his fingers through his short hair. Meg was one of the best things that ever happened to him. And one way or another, he would fix this.

Chapter 8

Meg heard the car pull into her driveway and looked out her bedroom window. Ethan sat in his car for a couple of minutes before he finally stepped out. She touched her hand to the glass. He looked tired. Even from her vantage point, she could see he hadn't slept nearly enough. Maybe she could fix that.

She trotted down the stairs and opened the front door just as Ethan raised his hand to knock.

"Come in." Meg stood on tiptoe and kissed his rough cheek.

He smiled tiredly. "Hell of a greeting, woman." His blue eyes moved from the top of her head down to her bare feet. She wore a simple baby blue velour suit with matching nail polish. "You look lovely today."

Meg patted her fine hair secured tightly in her ponytail and chuckled. "I have a magazine layout later." She hooked her arm around Ethan's waist and guided him inside. "Are you sure you want to do this today? You look rather tired."

"Wouldn't miss it." Ethan glanced at the gold watch on his wrist. "We've got about fifteen minutes before Brad arrives. How about a cup of coffee?"

"My pleasure." Meg led him into the kitchen and pulled a chair back for him to sit in. Then she rummaged around in her cabinets until she found the expensive coffee that she saved for a luncheon at the office or a business meeting.

She turned on her coffeemaker and sat across from Ethan. His casual yellow shirt and blue jeans couldn't hide the fact he was dead on his feet.

"You work too hard."

Ethan's head swiveled quickly to meet Meg's eyes. He smiled. "Occupational hazard."

"My dad used to say that balance was the key. You can't squeeze more hours from the day that God gave you."

"Wise man." Ethan placed his hand on top of Meg's and squeezed gently.

"He was." Meg bit down on the urge to share more information with Ethan. She would wait until this weekend to talk about her past and her parents. And all the misconceptions surrounding one of the worst periods of her life. She stood up and shuffled over to the refrigerator.

"I've made sandwiches and snacks." Meg looked over at Ethan and smiled. "I'm convinced that's half the reason Brad comes over here to study." She poured Ethan a cup of coffee and placed it in front of him.

He took the cup gratefully and sipped the dark brew. His blue eyes opened wide. "Good God, this is great coffee! What kind is it?"

Meg told him and put the bag of beans on the table. "Take it with you. I have lots more in the cabinets."

"Thanks." Ethan opened his mouth to say something else when Meg heard a knock at the front door.

"Hold that thought." She walked around to his side of the table and kissed his forehead softly before she left the room.

Meg opened the front door and smiled at the teenager. "Come in, Brad. We're both in the kitchen."

The gangly teen stepped inside. "Ethan's here?"

"Sure." Meg looked at him in surprise. "He told you he'd be here, right?"

"Yeah." Brad shrugged. But Meg saw the relief in his eyes, and her heart lurched. Ethan was exactly the person Brad needed in his life. A man who kept his word.

"Come on." Meg fought the urge to sling her arm around Brad's shoulder. "You can pick out a snack in the kitchen and take it to the library with you."

They walked down the hallway and into the kitchen.

"Hey, man!" Brad sauntered over to the table and picked up three sandwiches from the plate. "Don't think you can come here and eat all my food."

Ethan smiled cockily. "Privileges of the adult world. Didn't you get the memo?"

Brad chuckled and jerked his head toward the library. "I haven't got all day. You coming?"

"I'm coming." Ethan pushed back from the table and leaned down to grab his coffee mug. He smiled and winked at Meg.

She watched the two males leave and sighed. She could get used to that. The testosterone filtered through her hallways even now. Meg rolled her eyes and sat down with a blank sheet of paper and a head full of thoughts.

* * * *

An hour later, she could clearly hear the laughter coming from the library and didn't want to interrupt. Meg smiled and put her pen down for a minute. It was uncomplicated. People simply enjoying each other's company.

The way she enjoyed Ethan.

Meg sighed. And she enjoyed Ethan a lot.

What if she scared him? Ran him off? Made him regret ever meeting her? She blew out a breath and looked at the clock. Brad's session was almost over. And she still wanted to help Ethan relax and rest. His job seemed to be eating him alive. And it wasn't doing him any favors.

Driven is good. Driven to the point of exhaustion...not so hot.

Meg heard the familiar voices growing stronger, and she shoved her notebook and pen into the nearest drawer. She snagged two sodas from the fridge and placed them on the table.

Brad walked in first, shaking his head. "I don't believe a word of it." He snagged the soda off the table with no wasted motion and popped the top.

Ethan trailed in next. He grabbed his soda and never broke eye contact with Brad. "I've got the police report to prove it."

"Police report?" Meg repeated faintly.

The two males turned to her and grinned.

"Seems the genius scientist here actually blew up a chemistry lab in college." Brad snickered and pointed at Ethan.

"You blew up a lab?" Her blue eyes widened.

"Yep." He grinned sheepishly. "I put one too many parts in." Ethan chuckled. "Singed my eyebrows smooth off."

Meg bit her lip to keep from laughing, but Brad had no such compunction. He rolled with laughter.

"You're too much, man. Too much." He drained the rest of his soda and made a two-point shot to the trash can by the back door. Brad nodded in satisfaction and turned back to the adults.

"I gotta go. Mom'll be here soon."

Meg shook her head at Ethan and followed Brad into the hallway. "Good day?"

"Not bad." He motioned to the kitchen doorway where Ethan now stood. "I wouldn't let boy wonder mess around in your kitchen." Brad threw his head back and laughed heartily.

"You're simply not right." Ethan moved forward and clapped the young man on his back. "And there will be retribution."

"Looking forward to it." Brad smiled at him and turned to walk to the driveway where his mother waited.

Meg watched him get into the car and exit her driveway. She turned and opened her mouth to make a smart-ass comment when Ethan's mouth molded to hers.

Every remark and thought left her head as his tongue moved expertly in her mouth and made her ache. Her arms wound around his neck as she pressed herself fully to him.

Meg's nipples throbbed. When she pressed as close as she could against Ethan's chest, he groaned.

His mouth moved away for a second. "Have I told you how much I love to feel your body next to mine?"

"Not today." Meg smiled. "But we can go upstairs, and you can tell me again."

She shut the front door and slipped her small hand into his large one. Meg led him upstairs to her bedroom. When she turned into him, Ethan pulled her hair loose and thrust his fingers into the sable silkiness. His mouth met hers, and he tasted every inch of her.

"And did I tell you that I love the way you taste?" Ethan nibbled on her bottom lip and sucked the fullness into his mouth. His hands moved on her waist right under the hem of her top.

Meg moaned and tried to move as close as possible into him. "You look tired."

Ethan chuckled. "Not that tired." His hands moved up and cupped her full breasts.

She sighed in pleasure as he unhooked her bra and moved his hands back to her bare flesh. Then he lifted her shirt and bent his head to take her nipple deeply into his mouth. His tongue flicked back and forth against her aching nipple.

Meg clutched his red hair tightly as he moved from one breast to the other. Ethan lifted his head and moved his hands down to her waist. Then he turned and fell on the bed with her on top of him.

She blinked and then laughed. Meg sat astride Ethan, and he looked up at her with a grin.

"That was smooth."

"Thanks." He moved his hands up to her waist again.

Meg pulled her shirt and bra off. She sat with her legs on either side of Ethan as he looked up at her. Then she leaned forward and brushed her nipple against his lips.

"I suppose I'm running this show?" She jerked her body tightly against his hard cock.

"Was there any doubt?" Ethan's breath wheezed out on a strangled moan. He latched onto her nipple and moved his hand up to cup the other one.

Meg moved her hand down between them and stroked his cock through his pants. As she fit her pussy against it, she wiggled her hips down on him.

Ethan closed his eyes with a groan. "Too many clothes."

"Maybe." Meg moved slowly down his body to the end of the bed. In one smooth motion, she pulled her pants and panties off.

He sat up on his elbows and watched her.

Meg moved forward and crawled back on the bed. She pulled Ethan to a sitting position and pulled his yellow shirt off with barely a pause. Immediately he moved his hands down to her ass and clutched her tightly.

"Meg," he breathed against her breasts.

"Yes." She removed his hands and slid back down his body. Meg bent forward and brushed her soft hair against his stomach. When his body tightened, she chuckled.

She undid the buttons of his jeans, and he lifted his ass to help her slide them off.

Meg pulled his jeans off and let them drop to the floor. Slowly she trailed her hands up Ethan's legs until she reached the bottom of his boxer briefs. His eager cock strained against the fabric.

He reached for her, and she pushed his hands back down. Then she bent and brushed her lips softly against his cock. She watched as Ethan's hands clenched on her bedspread and smiled.

Meg bent forward and placed her hands on his thighs while she brushed her breasts against his balls.

"Meg," he wheezed. As he looked at her, his blue eyes darkened to cobalt. "You're torturing me."

"Maybe." She reveled in the power she had over his eager body. She lifted his waistband and moved it down just enough to see Ethan's cock head appear. Meg looked up at Ethan and licked her lips. Then she placed the tip of him in her mouth and flicked her tongue against him.

The soft hardness responded willingly to her touch. Ethan arched his hips up to ease more of his hard cock into her soft mouth. She licked and sucked his hard length for several minutes as Ethan groaned and arched upwards. Meg pulled his underwear down farther and moved her mouth away from him for a minute.

"My turn." Ethan reached for her, but she smiled and dropped his underwear on the floor.

"I'll let you know when it's your turn," Meg promised. She crawled back on the bed and straddled his lap. She spread her legs over his cock but didn't let Ethan slide into her. She moved his cock so it rubbed against her swollen clit. In a slow rhythm Meg moved against him.

Ethan's hands moved up to clutch her hips. He threw back his head and arched against her.

"You're so hot. I can feel you."

His words excited Meg, and she smiled. She moved slowly up to his waist and looked down at him. "Do you want your turn?"

"Yes." Ethan's voice was hoarse.

Inch by inch Meg moved up until her pussy was directly above Ethan's mouth. She lowered herself down willingly and cried out as he grabbed her ass and moved his tongue against her pussy folds. She was open to anything he wanted to do to her, and Ethan licked and sucked her deeply.

She grabbed the headboard and worked her pussy against Ethan's mouth as he found her clit and sucked it in a steady rhythm. Her body trembled at the sensations.

Meg moved against Ethan's mouth as he fucked her with his tongue. She moved her left hand from the headboard to her nipple and plucked at the swollen nub. As Ethan's tongue flicked against her, her body shook.

She trembled as her orgasm began to build. Ethan's hands clutched her ass as he ate her relentlessly.

Meg arched her back and cried out as she came with a fierceness that left her blind and deaf to everything but the spasms that took over her body. Shuddering, she struggled to breathe.

To give herself a respite from the pleasure Ethan gave to her she moved down a bit. His hands still gripped her hips, and he slid her slowly down his body. Meg moaned in pleasure at the feel of the tip of his cock penetrating her wet pussy.

As Ethan slid his full length inside her, he stretched her to the limit. He grabbed her hips and moved slowly in and out. As he thrust, he kept his body tightly against hers and Meg trembled as his body brushed against her aching clit time after time.

"Meg," Ethan whispered against her hair. He groaned as she sped up the pace and he let her take over the rhythm.

She licked her lips and arched against him with a force that knocked him back further onto the bed. With a single-minded purpose she jerked her hips and smiled as his breathing became harsh and uneven.

"Come for me, Ethan." She smiled down at him.

His hands clenched on her bare skin. "You're killing me."

Meg leaned down farther and let her hair brush against his body. "Come for me," she whispered.

As he surged over and over into her Ethan groaned and clutched her hips. Meg threw her head back and cried out as she came again while Ethan moved beneath her. His body stiffened, and he shouted aloud seconds later.

She collapsed against his hard chest and sighed. Then Ethan threaded his fingers through her hair and leaned up to kiss her forehead.

"I haven't been so relaxed in days."

Meg shifted a bit so she could look into his eyes. "Why don't you stay? Take a load off your mind for a while."

Ethan shook his head with a grimace. "Can't. Though I appreciate the offer. As soon as I get this little problem ironed out, I'll be sure and take you up on that."

"Raincheck, again?" she teased.

"I want to run a tab, woman." Ethan chuckled and traced Meg's lips with his fingers.

She grinned. "I may make that happen." Meg started to move then changed her mind. "I'm staying right here." She brushed her hair back out of her face. "If you can get out from underneath me, I might let you go." Her blue eyes sparkled.

"Woman!"

Meg tapped her fingers against Ethan's bare chest. "Don't overtax yourself."

"I'll stay for just a while longer." Ethan moved his hand down her body and grabbed the side of the sheet. Once he brought it over both of them, he closed his eyes.

She heard him sigh softly once before his breathing evened out. Meg sighed contentedly and curled up closer on his chest. She would deal with her mess tomorrow. Right now, she would take this moment of peace and savor it.

Meg closed her eyes and fell into a deep slumber.

* * * *

Ethan woke with a start. He had been having a nightmare of monumental proportions. His hand moved wearily up to his eyes and rubbed the sleep from them, and his heart pounded in his chest. He and the experiment had been beating the holy hell out of each other while Meg was tied to a bed. Winner takes all. The dream was bad enough. But then, he belatedly realized he was losing.

Ethan stroked Meg's silky hair that lay across his chest. Her bare breasts pressed to his side. He would love nothing more than to lay in bed with her all day, but he couldn't. If he didn't get the experiment fixed, and soon, Ethan feared that his world would implode.

He glanced over and saw the little black box peeking out from the edge of a colorful scarf beside the bed. A pang of jealousy tore through him. Did Meg cry out in pleasure with the toy as she did with him? The proof was in his study. He knew she did.

Ethan had the insane urge to shove those earrings through his ear, never mind the fact his ears weren't pierced, and have it out with the toy. The anger passed slowly, and he tried to relax.

They would have the toy back soon enough. Then he and Meg could move on with their relationship. And that was more important right now than a damn black box that haunted every aspect of his life.

Who would have thought that potentially bringing a woman pleasure could damn near ruin his life?

* * * *

Meg woke around nine and noted that there wasn't a hard chest beneath her head, but a soft bed. She opened one blue eye blearily and stretched like a cat. She would have preferred the chest. And Meg would be sure to let Ethan know the next time she saw him.

She smiled and tucked the sheet over her breasts. *Ethan*. Nice way to spend the evening. And the morning. And most everything in between. Meg bit her lip as her long day stretched out before her. She couldn't put it off any longer. She and Colin Price were due for a meeting. One which would undoubtedly change his little world forever.

Meg stood and walked over to her closet. She would wear her red suit. It was a powerful color, and she needed all the help she could get right now.

She'd pull her hair up and wear the high heels. Red lipstick. Colors and visuals to convey she wasn't a woman to trifle with.

"Arrogant bastard," she muttered.

Meg sighed as she glanced over at the black box on her nightstand. She would miss Derek. But then again, she pretty much had a closet full of Dereks. Didn't she? The damn toy needed a disclaimer on it or something. Warn a woman before activating a humanistic toy that developed feelings.

And that's what really pissed her off. *Who does this Colin guy think he is? God or something? Creating a toy that could feel? That could emote?*

She glanced at the black box again and grimaced. Derek deserved someone, too. Maybe another nice, little black box with female circuits. Meg smiled ruefully. She'd be sure to bring that up. After she tore Colin a new asshole.

* * * *

Meg drove her black SUV to the building she came to only weeks earlier. It was large, brick and nondescript.

She scowled as she turned the vehicle off. Perfect place to fuck with a person's life and seemingly get away with it.

She stepped out and pulled her jacket down with a brisk snap. Her jet-black hair tucked tightly against her head. By God, balls would be snipped this day. And heaven help the stupid male who tried to back-peddle and make it all right.

Meg locked her door and strode purposefully to the front door. No one expected her. And that made everything even better. She had been ambushed. And now it was her turn.

The door opened easily, and Meg stepped inside the massive lobby. Her heels clicked on the floor as she advanced toward the elevator. She pressed the button and waited for the doors to open. Once they did, she stepped inside and pressed the number five.

Meg's stomach clenched with nerves, and she willed herself to calm down. She couldn't afford to lose control and act like an idiot in this situation. All those years of protecting her family's name and who she was strengthened her resolve.

It had been extremely difficult to hold her head high when the rumors began to circulate after her parents' death. The reports that hinted at a murder/suicide. Gossipy reporters that latched onto the worst moment of her life and magnified it for the world to see.

Insinuations of drug use and greed. Infidelity. And information leaked to whip up the frenzied public.

Meg drew in a shaky breath. Erica stood by her the entire time. The rest of her family distanced themselves from the stories. Left Meg to fend for herself after being orphaned. And those things had helped shape who she was. What she was made of. And she swore that she would never blacken her parents' name. Never again mar their memory.

The elevator doors slid open, and Meg exhaled and stepped out. She glanced to the left and then the right. Colin was around here somewhere. Probably holed up somewhere jerking off to her tapes with Derek. The thought both infuriated and fueled her. *Oh, it was on.* And heaven help the unsuspecting male.

Meg walked down the long corridor with her heels tapping on the bare floor. She sniffed disdainfully. It smelled of cleaning supplies and sterility. Almost like a hospital. She grimaced.

She began to open doors. A storage room. The next door, a small room with a table and four chairs. Meg recognized it from her previous meeting. Her left hand clenched into a tight fist before she found some semblance of control and eased back.

There were only two more doors before the hallway curved to her right. She tried both. Nothing. Meg turned the corner and bared her teeth. There was a large door straight ahead. And she would bet that it housed a certain unethical piece of shit named Colin Price.

Meg walked purposefully forward and didn't stop a second to think about her actions or her words. Instead she simply grasped the doorknob and swung it open with enough force to leave it slamming against the wall.

She watched in satisfaction as Colin's head jerked up with wide eyes and an open mouth.

"Hi, honey." Meg slammed her hands flat on the table he worked at. "I'm home."

He was confused. Meg saw it and smiled in satisfaction.

"Jesus!" Colin stood upright and raked his hands through his hair. "You scared the shit out of me. I suppose it would have been too much to ask to pick up a damn phone or something."

Meg's eyes narrowed. "Oh no. This called for a one-on-one interview. A meeting of the minds, so to speak."

"Say what you have to say." Colin grimaced. "You haven't liked me from the beginning. A fact I truly don't understand." He sighed. "And when I came to you and your partner with a wonderful business proposition, you shut me down with no explanation whatsoever. I deserve something, at least."

"You deserve something?" Meg repeated the words in disbelief. "You fucking deserve something?" she growled low in her throat, and her blue eyes shot sparks. "You deserve to have your nuts snipped, your dick chopped off and stuck up your ass. That's what you deserve!"

Colin flew back from the desk at a rapid rate of speed. His chair hit the wall, and he stood in one, smooth motion.

"You're a fucking lunatic."

He struggled to remain calm in the face of an insane woman in his office. Meg would have laughed if she hadn't been so furious.

"You are pathetic," Meg snarled at him. "Tricking a woman into an experiment and not divulging all the details."

The color drained from his face quickly. And Colin struggled to stay in control. "I have no idea what you're talking about, Ms. Whittington."

"You're a pitiful liar, Mr. Price." Meg mocked him with a pleasant smile. "And don't think for a minute I don't know that millions of my dollars have been invested in this project." Realization hit, and she paused. "You haven't seen the tapes?"

"No." The word was curt. "I haven't. But I assure you, the woman involved in the experiment signed consent forms." His brown eyes narrowed. "So whatever pieces you've heard about the experiment are undoubtedly lies. A feeble attempt from the woman to extort money."

Meg walked around the side of the desk and punched Colin square in his nose. Then she watched in satisfaction as he doubled over and wheezed while cupping his bleeding nose.

"Jesus!" He moved backwards away from her with one hand trying to keep distance between them.

"He won't help you now." Meg waited until Colin straightened a bit and looked at her. She leaned down close.

"I *am* that woman, you son of a bitch."

Fear danced across Colin's features. "Impossible," he muttered.

Meg injected a southern lilt into her speech. "Why, sugar. You have no idea who you're dealing with."

"You tricked me!" He pulled a handkerchief from his pocket and held it to his dripping nose. "You bitch!"

"Tricked you?" Meg snarled. "I ought to have you blackballed. Let me reiterate." She slammed her hand down on the table again. "You will cease with this fucking project. You will somehow fix this clusterfuck you've created. And you will not mention a word of this to anyone. Failure to adhere to these guidelines will give me license to fuck your little world with no lubricant. Got it?"

Colin grimaced. "You're killing my project because you like to spread your legs? I thought a woman like you would love it. I haven't seen the tapes, but I've seen the numbers. You've enjoyed every inch of the experiment's dick."

Meg flew at him with a growl and kicked and punched the shit out of him. He stumbled back against the onslaught, and the filing cabinet fell over. She continued to elude his punches while truly beating the shit out of him. All those years of self-defense classes came in handy.

One minute she was on top of Colin, and the next she was being lifted, kicking and screaming. One of Colin's wild punches landed on her cheek, and she growled. Her hands curved into claws as she struggled to move back to her prey.

"Let me go!" she demanded. Meg slammed her elbow into her captor's solar plexus and grinned at the *oomph* it produced. Then she slammed her heels into the man's toes. He let her go quickly, and she spun to around to get her bearings and proceed with beating his ass.

Meg looked at the man before her and frowned. The pain in her hands and cheek paled next to the feelings that flooded through her. She scowled.

"What are you doing here?"

Chapter 9

Meg watched in disbelief as Ethan bent and helped Colin off the floor. She stood stock-still and waited for an explanation. An explanation that would make this entire scene all right.

Because no way in hell was her boyfriend in this building. In this office. And helping that heap of shit off the floor. *No way.*

"Meg." Ethan moved toward her, and she moved quickly away.

He sighed.

"I can explain."

I can explain? Did he just say that he could explain? Meg frowned. She was in the midst of a nightmare. One that tore her world in shreds.

"I think I would love to hear that." Meg sat calmly in one of the chairs as if she hadn't beaten the shit out of Colin. As if the throbbing in her cheek didn't matter. She crossed her legs and waited.

Colin glared at her through his one good eye and opened his mouth, but Ethan waved his hand. Colin snapped his mouth shut and waited.

"Our experiment was never meant to harm. Only help."

Our?

"We wanted to simulate a woman's deepest fantasies to bring her pleasure. To satisfy her." He rubbed his hand across his forehead. "We didn't know the experiment would take on a life of its own."

"You knew?" Meg growled. "You fucking knew?"

"Please." Ethan held up his large hands. "Let me explain. And then we can try and work this out."

Meg's blue eyes narrowed. "Continue." She didn't take her eyes from Ethan's face. The lying face of the man she fell in love with. That hurt worse than her hands or her cheek.

"I've come across technology that will access a woman's pleasure zones in her brain. And convey them to a willing receptor." Ethan paced the small office. "We only wished to help. We had no idea the experiment would begin to emote."

Meg stood with as much dignity as she could muster. "You both used me. One for money and one for an easy fuck." Her blue eyes iced over as she stared into Ethan's eyes. "You must be the one who viewed the tapes. Who watched your experiment slide his cock into me over and over again. And you obviously thought it was a good idea to try a piece of that." She smiled and showed all her teeth. "Hope I didn't disappoint."

She turned and motioned to Colin. "And you needed the money. My money. To further this bullshit and push it onto the masses." Meg pointed at them both. "I'm running this show now, you bastards. And it will be something neither one of you will ever forget."

Ethan opened his mouth.

Meg winked at him and leaned closer. "If you want to continue to use that cock of yours, you'll shut your mouth and nod your head."

Ethan's mouth snapped shut, and he nodded his head once.

She straightened and looked at both men. "Pleasure doing business. I'll be back tomorrow with papers for each of you to sign. There is, after all, a matter of my privacy at stake." Meg looked both men in the eye, one after the other. "And then I'll be back to tell you how you're going to handle this fuck-up."

She held her hand up. "Not one fucking word out of either one of you." Meg turned and left the office with long strides.

* * * *

She actually drove two blocks, out of sight of the building, before she opened the door of her vehicle and threw up all over the road. Her hands trembled as she shut the door again and leaned back against the plush seat.

First, she would contact her lawyer and have him draw up papers. Meg felt the tears slide down her cheeks but paid them no heed. Not only had she lost her toy, she had lost her boyfriend, her self-esteem, and millions of dollars in one fell blow.

But it was the betrayal that cut the deepest. Ethan.

She closed her eyes and inhaled deeply. Ethan knew who she was. And he fucked her. Literally and figuratively.

Meg trusted him. *Trusted him!* How stupid was she? How hard up could she possibly be to fall for his shit? She shuddered and let the tears fall. Her cheek throbbed painfully, but she didn't care. She didn't give a shit about anything right this minute. And that, for once, was a blessing.

* * * *

Ethan practically shoved Colin into a chair as he turned to follow Meg.

"Don't," Colin's swollen mouth spit out the word.

Ethan looked back at his friend and grimaced in sympathy. Meg had royally fucked Colin up. He was a mass of black and blue bruises. His nose likely broken. One eye completely swollen shut. A knot on his forehead and a split lip.

But Ethan didn't particularly care right this minute. He knew he had fucked up. And he was still mad at Colin for hitting Meg.

"I have to fix this."

"Fix it?" Colin stood on shaky legs. "I'm suing the fucking bitch. Suing her rich ass."

"What?" Ethan's puzzlement was clear. "Are you delirious?"

"You've been fucking Margaret Elizabeth Whittington, and you didn't see fit to tell me?"

"What?" Ethan repeated.

"You're shitting me." Colin moved around the side of his desk slowly and looked up into Ethan's face. "Ah, fuck. You had no idea, did you?"

"I still have no idea what you're talking about." Ethan motioned to the door. "That's Meg White. The woman in the experiment. The woman I care about. I think you're confused."

Colin started to laugh but grimaced as pain shot through his mouth. "Damn it, Ethan! That is not Meg White! Her name is Margaret Elizabeth Whittington. She's on the board of directors that oversees our grant. And," Colin paused for effect, "she's obviously as insane as her father." He touched his mouth and winced.

"Sit down before you fall down." Ethan shoved him none too gently into a chair.

"If you paid any attention to the newsletters I send out, you would know who she is, dammit!"

"Start at the beginning," Ethan demanded.

"That woman who just left here is Margaret Elizabeth Whittington." Colin sighed. "Rich bitch of the world. A woman who is clearly insane and deadly." He motioned to his face. "You saw what she did to me."

"Quit whining and keep talking." Ethan crossed his arms over his chest and waited.

"I don't know what happened," Colin muttered. "The woman who picked up the device didn't look like her." He closed his one good eye and uttered one word. "Fuck. The sneaky bitch must have worn a disguise."

"What else, Colin?"

"She must be a closet nympho." Colin nodded. "Makes sense. Stocks up on sexual devices because she can't keep a man. Sad, really."

Ethan smiled and moved forward quickly. He balled his fist and hit Colin in his good eye and stepped back.

Colin howled in pain and clutched at his face.

"The next time you decide you have a foolproof plan, leave me out of it." He opened the door and walked back toward his office.

Not only was he a dating disaster, a magnet for mayhem, he was the fucking Titanic of relationships.

Ethan rubbed his hands across his eyes and sank into his office chair. Meg must think he was the sorriest piece of shit in the universe. He should have told her. The thought insinuated itself into his brain and wouldn't let loose. *Should have told her. Should have told her.*

"Son of a bitch." Ethan hit his desk with a strong blow that had the wood splintering where he hit. He didn't care about what Colin said. In fact, he tuned his friend out quickly. He didn't particularly care if Meg was a Black Widow in mortal form.

Ethan knew Meg. He tried the name "Margaret" aloud, but it didn't fit. He knew Meg. And yes, he had royally fucked her over for his job. Now, what was he going to do about it?

* * * *

Meg drove home slowly and called her lawyer on her cell. He promised to have the papers drawn up and delivered to her house within the hour. She snapped her cell shut and turned off the engine in her driveway.

Maybe she should have stuck to vibrators and dildos. Should have kept her emotions to herself and satisfied herself physically.

Meg set her jaw and stepped from the SUV. She wasn't done, yet. She would turn Derek in tomorrow. But tonight, he would fuck her brains out. He would use his tongue, hands, and cock to pleasure her until she couldn't think anymore. Didn't want to think anymore.

She stepped inside her home and locked the door behind her. Meg stripped in the hallway and walked naked up to her room. She slid the earrings in her ears and turned the box on.

Derek appeared instantly, and Meg sat on the edge of her bed. "Fuck me," she demanded.

His clothes disappeared in an instant, and he moved to cover her body with his. Meg clutched his shoulders and spread her legs eagerly. But Derek didn't slide into her. He simply rolled over to his side and cradled Meg's bare body close to his.

She struggled against his embrace and cursed. "I don't want affection, damn you. Fuck me. That's what I want. Now do it!"

"Meg." Derek brushed her hair back from her face and scowled. "What is this?" He touched the bruise softly. "Who hurt you?"

"Everyone," she whispered. "Everyone hurt me." Her head dropped forward onto Derek's chest, and she struggled to keep her composure. When she lifted her head, her blue eyes glistened with unshed tears. "Just fuck me, Derek. Okay? Don't think. Don't question me. It's what I need right now. Please."

He sighed. "I'll give you what you need. I promise." He smiled and tugged her hair lightly. She moved her mouth up eagerly to meet his. But it wasn't a domination of his mouth on hers. His lips moved softly against her, and she trembled as she fought against losing control.

Derek moved his mouth from hers and rained tiny kisses over her swollen cheek to her ear. "Beautiful, strong Meg." His breath fanned her ear softly. "Every man's dream." His hand moved down to cup her breast. "With a heart made for love."

Meg shuddered at his words and leaned into him. "Please."

His other hand stroked her hair. "Tell me, Meg. Tell me. I can help."

And she told him.

* * * *

Meg dressed the next morning in a dark purple suit with matching pumps. She pulled her hair back and piled it on top of her head in a tight bun. Never again would she make the mistake of letting her guard down again with either of the men she was meeting this morning.

The papers her lawyer drew up were safely ensconced in her black briefcase. She would get in, make them sign the papers, and tell them exactly how they were going to handle the situation.

And she would keep Derek.

Damn Ethan to hell.

Obviously, a real man was a little too much to ask for. Or at least, a real honest man. Meg rubbed her temple and told herself that it would be over soon. All of it.

She applied her make-up with a heavy hand and stiffened her backbone. Meg studied her reflection in the mirror and frowned. She looked like some pompous matriarch millionaire. *Great.* At least neither man would think he could simply run the hell over her.

She smiled grimly. She knew damn good and well that Colin wouldn't. Meg hoped he was so fucking sore that he couldn't sleep for a week. *Arrogant bastard.*

But her feelings for Ethan were more complicated. *And isn't that just the worst thing of all?*

Meg growled and snatched the black briefcase off her bed. *Screw both of them.* She would get over this. Get over the hurt. The pain. The disappointment. She had to. There was no way that she would let this become an insurmountable setback. It was only her heart, after all.

* * * *

Meg drove her black SUV back to the building that housed the two rats and parked it in front. She removed the briefcase and locked her door. Then she strode purposefully into the building and took the elevator up to the correct floor. The doors opened, and she stepped out.

If memory served, then the men would be in Colin's office just around the corner. She took a deep breath and pushed onward. Her heels clicked hollowly on the floor, and she lifted her chin.

The door was open, and Meg didn't pause as she stepped inside.

"Ah. I see you're both here. Excellent."

Ethan's jaw dropped at her appearance.

"Yes?" she inquired. "Can I help you with something, or are you in the habit of catching flies?"

"Meg?"

"You may call me Ms. Whittington." She turned to Colin. He looked as if he were in a six-car pile-up. She smiled in satisfaction. "And how are you this morning, Mr. Price?"

"I feel like shit. As well you know."

"Yes. Pity that." Meg looked down into his battered face, and her grin widened. "Or not." She slammed her briefcase down on the table and popped the snaps. Meg picked up the sheaf of papers and slid them across to Colin. "You first." She glanced at Ethan. "Then him."

She thumbed through the stack. "Each is marked. Initial where indicated. Sign where indicated."

Colin snatched a pen out of his inner jacket pocket and began scribbling at the places that were marked.

Ethan stepped forward. "Meg. Please. We'll sign the papers. But I need to talk to you."

"You and I are done, Mr. Fields." She looked him in the eye. "And I've decided to keep the toy, thanks. He seems to be a lot less trouble than you are."

Colin's head shot up. "Like hell."

"Mr. Price, you really don't have a leg to stand on. My money made him. Your indiscretions have sealed the deal. He's mine. All mine. And you two won't be using research funds to make the same mistake again. I've seen to it." Meg motioned to the papers. "And you've agreed."

"Damn it, Meg!" Ethan slammed his fist against the wall. "Screw the research! You and I have to talk."

"Oh." Meg pulled out another stack of papers. "And this is a restraining order against you, Mr. Fields."

Ethan's blue eyes widened in shock, and Meg fought not to take back the papers and tear them up.

"I. See." He grabbed the papers from her hand and clenched them tightly in his fist. "Is that what you want? To keep a little black box to fuck when you could have a man who loves you?" He nodded at her sudden intake of breath. "Yes, Meg. Loves you."

"Mr. Fields." Meg fought to keep her voice steady. "This is inappropriate." She motioned to the papers. "This matter is finished." She looked back at Colin. "Return the papers to the address on the last sheet. You've got two days. I've got an appointment."

Ethan stood in front of her in the doorway. "Meg." His voice washed over her. "Talk to me. Please. I can't tell you how sorry I am. Let me make it up to you."

Meg's hand shot out, and she slapped him across the face. "Stay out of my life. That will make it up to me." She walked quickly out of the office and to the elevator. She wasn't stopped again.

* * * *

Meg's hands shook as she tried to put her key into the ignition. "Son of a bitch." The key finally slid home, and she started the SUV quickly and pulled out of the parking lot.

She needed to get home. As soon as possible. Before she completely broke down.

The restraining order may have been a low blow. But no lower than Ethan manipulating every situation to his favor.

She rubbed her temple and cursed the fates. *I am fine. I am fine.* Meg repeated the three little words until, somehow, she almost believed it.

Both men were out of her life for good. She would keep a close eye on any future projects Mr. Price had up his sleeve. No more hands-off funding. Look where it got her.

As for Ethan...who knew? She now had a legal right to call the police on him if he approached her. She took a shuddering breath. It was the only shield she had right now, and she wasn't above using it.

Her life had to go on. To continue without Ethan. How could she even remotely consider having him in her life now? He lied to her. She would simply take up where she left off before.

No harm. No foul.

* * * *

Meg woke up the next morning and dressed quickly in a light blue velour track suit. She would clean today before Brad came for his lesson. Never mind the pounding in her head or the hollow feeling in her stomach. She would never forgive herself if her fucked-up life affected one of her students.

The kitchen was a bit cool, and she slid on bright orange socks and proceeded to make a plateful of sandwiches. There was enough soda so she didn't have to worry about Brad moaning about lack of caffeine. But she had no idea what to do when he would ask her about Ethan. And he would.

How unfair to bring a steadfast male into his life only to snatch him out later. Meg winced. Maybe she could look into a professor from the college or high school that wanted a little part-time work on the side. And she would check this one's references.

She placed the turkey and ham on the sandwiches while her mind wandered over the rest of her day. It would be a long one. Meg only scheduled Brad this afternoon. With no other plans looming on the horizon, she would probably curl up with a book and bemoan her life.

The knock on the door startled her, and she frowned. Meg glanced at the clock and shook her head. That boy ran on his own time. But he had never been this early before. She rinsed off her hands and dried them quickly on a hand towel.

Meg hurried down the hall and flung the door open. The greeting died on her lips as she stared up into Ethan's face. She turned on her heel and started to slam the door behind her. But it never made a satisfying smack. She turned back around with eyes narrowed.

Ethan stepped into her foyer and studied her with intense blue eyes.

"Get out," she demanded. "I'll call the police."

"Brad has a lesson today." Ethan shrugged out of his brown coat and hung it on the coatrack. "I believe we can put our differences aside for a couple of hours for the young man."

"Our differences?" Meg's eyes blazed. "Is that the euphemism we're using now?" She scowled. "And I thought your associate was the arrogant one."

"Colin has his issues." Ethan sighed and held out his hands. "Please, Meg. I don't want to disappoint him."

She lifted her chin. "Fine. You can stay for the lesson. And then you leave. And as soon as I find a replacement, you are never to darken my doorway again. Got it?"

He nodded stiffly.

"You can wait in the kitchen. I don't want you wandering around in my house."

Meg walked into the kitchen and sat at the table. She finished making the sandwiches and slid them into the fridge. She sat back down and sipped her soda. Ethan sat across from her and studied her face.

"I'm sorry."

The apology ripped through her, and she shrugged lightly. "The deed is done, Ethan."

"I'm sorry I hurt you." Ethan pinned her with his gaze. "I'm sorry I didn't tell you from the beginning what I was doing."

Meg started to stand, but he clasped her hands in his. "I'm sorry that I used you for research when all I really wanted to do was to get to know you better." He sighed. "I'm sorry I squandered every opportunity to start this relationship with trust."

Her throat clogged, and she cleared it quickly.

"I'm sorry, Meg." Ethan brought her hands to his lips and softly kissed them. "I love you."

She removed her hands. "Words, Ethan. A lot of words. And you seem to be quite good at stringing them together to get what you want." Meg looked him square in the eye. "I have the Ultimate Sex Toy, remember?" She grinned with no humor whatsoever. "What else does a nympho like me need?"

Meg stood and pushed her chair in. "By the way, Derek can block any and all attempts from you to access his audio and visual. So give it up." Her lips tightened into a flat line. "All of it."

Ethan raked his hands through his short, red hair. "Tell me what to do to make it right. I'll do anything." His blue eyes begged for forgiveness.

The doorbell rang, and Meg shook her head. "Brad's here. I'll send him into the study."

Ethan stood and walked out of the kitchen.

Meg took a deep, steadying breath and walked quickly to the front door. She opened it with a smile. The first genuine one of the day. The teenager stood there with his shaggy hair and ripped blue jeans.

"Ah. My first victim, er, student of the day."

He snickered. "Yeah. Yeah." He stepped inside. "I'm a little thirsty. Got something to drink?"

Meg slung her arm around his shoulder. "Something with caffeine that comes in a small aluminum can, perhaps?"

"Maybe." Brad grinned and let her escort him into the kitchen.

He looked around a bit in the hallway, and Meg inwardly sighed. Finding a replacement for Ethan in Brad's life was going to be about as hard as finding a replacement in hers. Should she be inclined to do that. Which, damn it all, she wasn't.

Meg put the can on the table, and Brad promptly palmed it and turned back toward the hallway. She sank down to the kitchen table and put her head in her hands.

Ethan's words played over and over again in her head.

But how could she trust him now? He had used her. Like some sexual guinea pig. And after all that time she gave him to confess what he was doing. Meg blinked back tears. How long had it been since she trusted somebody that much?

The question stuck in her mind, and she scowled. *Okay.* Maybe she hadn't trusted him with all the details. A family history and financial statement seemed to be lacking. But she hadn't lied to him.

Just her name.

Meg pinched the bridge of her nose and tried to ignore the persistent throbbing in her head. Ethan was bad. He was dishonest. He loved her.

"Shit," she muttered. Meg stood and pulled her hair back into a ponytail. She was going mad. Thoughts of Ethan flooded her brain. His hands on her. His words washing over her.

Maybe she should give him another chance. Maybe.

But with what guarantee?

There was no guarantee. Damn it! Just trust. An item that seemed to be sorely missing throughout their entire relationship.

"Hey!"

Meg's head shot up, and her heart raced.

Brad frowned at her. "You okay?"

"Sure." Meg waved her hand at him. "Just a bit of a headache. How was your lesson?"

"Cool." Brad walked over to the fridge and pulled out two sandwiches and another can of soda. "Can I take these with?"

"Help yourself." She stood and followed him out into the hallway. "I want to know what you make on that chapter test in science. Got me?"

"Yeah. I got ya." Brad smiled cockily. "If it's an 'A', will you make those cookies with the white chips in them?" He studied her hopefully.

"You can be charming when there's sugar on the line."

He waited.

"Sure." She uttered a small sigh of defeat. "What's a couple of hours slaving away in the kitchen when one of my favorite students makes an 'A'?"

"Thanks!" Brad opened the door and walked out to his mom's beaten down wagon. He climbed inside and waved as they drove off.

"And how charming do I have to be?"

Ethan's soft voice made goose bumps break out along her arms. She turned to him with a small smile. "I'd say you can be plenty charming, Mr. Fields. Wouldn't you?" Her eyes narrowed. "Charming enough to use me to suit yourself. How much charm does one man need?"

Meg growled low. "Or are you hoping to sweet talk me into giving you back the toy?"

"Fuck the toy," Ethan said crudely. "I don't give a good goddamn if I ever see that black box again." He grabbed Meg by the arms and brought her closer to him. "You've brought me to my knees." His blue eyes searched hers. "I will give anything you want to get you back.

226

Anything. I don't care about the research. Or my job. Or anything. Just you." He smoothed her hair back. "Only you."

"Pretty words," she said shakily.

"True words. Honest words." His hands slid down, and he picked up one of hers. He lifted it and placed it on his chest. "I love you, Meg."

"I'm Margaret Elizabeth Whittington." She looked him in the eye. "They say my father killed my mother. That I'm from a cursed line. I have no family. No relatives. No one to give a damn." She paused. "And the one person I trusted my heart with used it for target practice."

"He's a bastard." Ethan kissed her gently on the forehead. "And he'll spend the rest of his life making it up to you."

"How can I trust him?" Meg cocked her head to the side. "Why should I? When I have a toy that will do whatever I say?"

"You need a man, Meg. A flesh-and-blood being that would lay down his life for you." Ethan cupped her cheek. "I'm that man."

She stepped back. "And what do you propose I do with Derek? Dismantle him? Recycle him?"

"No." Ethan bit his lip. "There has to be someone who could care for him. Someone who can be his world."

"And if I want it to be me?"

Ethan's eyes flared with jealousy, and he clenched his jaw. "Then I will gladly step aside."

"Would you?" she asked softly. "Step aside for your creation?"

"If it would make you happy," Ethan nodded glumly, "then I would."

Meg slid her hand in his and tugged him gently toward her. She walked to the stairs and led Ethan up to her room.

"What good is a man who can't pick out a can of tomatoes?" Meg smiled softly and turned to him inside her doorway.

"You can teach me." Ethan stopped just shy of the entrance. "But I won't be second fiddle to a projection." He motioned to the nightstand where her scarf covered a box. His eyes narrowed.

"Do you take direction well?" Meg pulled off her shirt and threw it on the floor.

Ethan's eyes gravitated toward her black, lacy bra. "I'm a man, Meg. Not a machine. With thoughts and feelings of my own." His blue eyes darkened. "But I wouldn't mind taking direction in the bedroom."

"Good." Meg stood on one leg and stepped out of one pant leg and then the other. "Because I gave Derek to Erica."

"You *gave* it away?"

She arched an eyebrow. "Yes. Problems with that?"

"No."

Meg smiled. There was no hesitation in his voice.

He stepped inside her bedroom.

"I'm a millionaire. I'm hard-headed and domineering." Meg put her hands on her hips. "I don't take shit from anyone, and I don't trust easily."

Ethan unbuttoned his shirt. "I wouldn't know the correct can of tomatoes if it bit me on the ass. I'm a scientist. A man who knows more about formulas than relationships. And one who, apparently, loves a certain stubborn woman."

Meg moved forward and reached up to tug at his short red hair. He bent his head, and she whispered in his ear, "We're obviously made for each other." She kissed his neck as she moved away. "And I have an idea for a few experiments of my own."

* * * *

Erica moaned as his cock slid in and out of her. She could feel her orgasm build with his sure, smooth strokes.

He grabbed her ass and rammed into her over and over again.

She cried out as her body convulsed tightly, and she arched up from the bed. Erica came back down slowly and sighed as she felt him stroke her body.

"You're perfect." Erica smiled and stroked his hair back from his forehead. "I had a friend tell me that I would finally find someone who could make my body sing."

"Wise friend." Colin smiled and covered her body with his again.

ABOUT THE AUTHOR

C'ann Inman is the pen name of Oklahoma author Crystal Inman.

She loves to spin wild and wicked stories for her readers. She realizes that romance can be found in many places and many ways. Her stories celebrate the sensuality of relationships.

Programmed for Pleasure is her second full-length release. It answers the question: What would you do with the Ultimate Sex Toy?

Keep track of Crystal/C'ann at
https://inmanbooks.com/
https://inmanbooks.blogspot.com/
https://www.facebook.com/inmanbooks